IRON

THE QUEEN & THE ASSASSIN

LISETTE MARSHALL

ISBN: 9789083256832

Cover design: 100Covers
Editor: Jennifer Lopez, Mistress Editing

www.lisettemarshall.com
www.facebook.com/LisetteMarshallAuthor
www.instagram.com/LisetteMarshallAuthor

CONTENTS

CONTENT NOTE

Like most of my books, *Iron* is a steamy, stabby fantasy romance. If that's all you need to know before you dive in, enjoy! If, on the other hand, you'd like to get a few more details before you start reading, check out the content warnings below.

Iron portrays occasional violence, and contains mentions of domestic violence in the past (none of it very graphic). The book contains multiple sex scenes (definitely graphic and fully consensual).

As the first book in a trilogy, it is not a standalone; however, it ends on a Happy For Now and there are no cliffhangers.

PROLOGUE

The duke of Sapphire Hill was a bore in bed.

A pity, because the man's seduction campaign was commendable. Flowers and bottles of wine. Smooth compliments at dinner. A couple of friends making unsubtle references to his honourable character. If he had put even a tenth of the effort into the result of his labours, the night might have progressed quite pleasantly for everyone involved.

Unfortunately, Tamar concluded mere minutes after the first kiss, Lord Pridon appeared to have declared his mission accomplished as soon as she invited him to her room.

Now she lay back in the silk and satin of her bed and thought about tomorrow's breakfast while he thrust away between her legs, panting and grimacing. Eggs – scrambled or cooked? Or perhaps she shouldn't pick eggs at all – she might as well grant herself a little treat to make up for this disappointment. Pancakes? It had been a while since she'd had pancakes...

Above her, the duke growled to a sudden climax and collapsed on top of her. Tamar absently patted him on the shoulder. Thank the gods he didn't compensate his lack of consideration with excessive stamina – imagine she'd have been lying here for an hour. Now it was a matter of preventing any further continuation of the dreariness... But at least she'd perfected the skill of kicking people out without too much of a hassle. A quick gesture sufficed to interrupt the usual blathering about what an honour and such a delight and was there anything else he could do to please her?

Not much use in telling him he should have started an hour earlier if he was trying to please her, Tamar knew from experience. She had made some attempts with the first men she allowed into her bedroom and concluded quickly it was a waste of effort: the type of man who believed himself enchanting enough to stick it in without further introduction was usually also the type to take constructive criticism quite badly.

'I appreciate the thought,' she said absently, nudging his naked body off her, 'but I'm content, thank you.'

'Well.' His chuckle came with a sense of awkwardness, as if he had expected she'd melt into a frenzy of admiration beneath him, and wasn't sure how to progress now that she remained solid. 'A glass of wine, perhaps? I could use—'

'No, thank you,' Tamar said, sitting up and reaching for her peignoir. 'I'm quite spent. Early appointments tomorrow morning, you know how it goes. Feel free to take that bottle with you when you leave.'

Only now did it appear to get through to him that a host of flowers might not be enough to compensate for the fact that he'd treated her like little more than a convenient hole from the moment he undressed her. The realisation slid over his smooth face with a sudden sharpness, the expression of a man who habitually reacts to a defeat by looking for someone else to blame.

'I'll be saving it for our next meeting, then,' he said, smiling with too much determination, a warning not to spoil his good mood. Unfortunately, all that smile achieved in Tamar was a sudden, violent desire to spoil his mood as thoroughly as humanly possible.

'I hope it ages well, my lord.'

'What in the...' He restrained himself just in time. 'I hope I'm misunderstanding you. It seems – after all my efforts – you must at least grant me a chance to extend our...'

'Must I?'

Pridon didn't hear the warning, or if he did hear it, he interpreted it as a challenge. With a sharp laugh, he said, 'Well, it would be highly unfortunate if anyone were to hear of our little tryst, wouldn't you—'

He caught her look and abruptly swallowed the rest of his words. Tamar slowly, very slowly raised her eyebrows as she wrapped her peignoir around her body without releasing his gaze. Sitting at the edge of her bed, the duke turned a greenish shade of pale.

'Yes,' she said, with deliberate pensiveness. 'Yes, I do agree that would be highly unfortunate indeed.'

He suddenly seemed in a hurry to gather his expensive silk clothes. 'Well – yes – so of course I will make sure nobody hears—'

'Wise.'

'I – I'll leave you alone, then.'

'Excellent.'

'And If you would like to meet again at any point in the future—'

'Wouldn't wait for it.'

He bowed, the bundle of clothes in his arms, and hurried through the connecting door in the corner of her bedroom – leading to the string of empty rooms through which she could smuggle her visitors in unnoticed. Tamar sent a last icy smile after him, closed the door and locked it. The bottle of wine, she found as she turned back to her room, remained on the nightstand.

Well. At least one pleasant surprise this evening.

She poured herself a glass, sank down on the edge of the bed, and closed her eyes. Her body felt used and tired, and not in the pleasant way – the duke's sweaty touch still sticking to her skin, his wet kiss lingering on her lips even after a few sips of the heavy red wine.

For hell's sake. Was there really not a decent man to be found in the entirety of Redwood? Or did only the wrong ones find their way to her room?

She should probably just stop inviting them altogether, she concluded as she planted the wine back onto her nightstand, sank back into the blankets, and slipped her fingers underneath her peignoir. At least she never disappointed herself. But a woman could hope –

Even a queen of iron, it turned out, could hope.

CHAPTER I

'Look, brother,' Runo said, taking a sip of his beer as he leaned back in his seat and draped his free arm over the back of the next chair. 'Don't take this personally, but you *have* to admit you're not making the most trustworthy of impressions at the moment.'

His conversation partner stared back at him without an answer. That was to say, Runo *assumed* the man stared back at him, but in the shadow of that oversized hood, from behind a black mask that covered most of the other's face, even that was hard to say for sure.

'They have this saying in Raulinna,' he cheerfully continued. 'A man hiding his face is a man hiding his intentions. Or he's just ugly, I suppose, but the proverbs never seem to take plain vanity into account. Anyway, assuming you're not some hideous monster, I'm going to conclude there's something you don't want me to know about you. Which, I must say, is unfortunate if I'm going to risk my neck based only on your cryptic reassurances.'

'Cryptic?' The other man scoffed. He spoke in Taavi, and quite fluently so, although his accent betrayed his Redwood birth. 'You seem to forget your Empress herself found me trustworthy enough to make use of my offer and send you to the north.'

'Sure she did,' Runo said. 'It's not her neck.'

Another short silence fell. At the other side of the taproom, some girls in short skirts were flocking around a company of gamblers. Closer to the door, a few old men were singing along with a badly tuned mandolin that sounded like it ached to kill the fellow playing it. Around the long table where he and his masked companion sat, however, the room remained suspiciously quiet.

A masked stranger silencing an entire tavern around him. Well, well. Runo took another sip, because beer tasted better than the feeling of not having much more to say, and waited. At long last, his conversation partner clucked his tongue and grumbled, 'So what did you want to know?'

'This thing.' Runo nodded at the small, slightly rusty key that lay between them on the table. 'Where does it come from?'

'My pocket.'

'Thanks, clever boy. How did it get *into* your pocket?'

'None of your concern.' The other's voice turned sharper, and suddenly it no longer sounded nearly as deep and gruff as a moment before. Was the man deliberately altering his voice? Quite interesting – it suggested the possibility they may still run into each other at another moment, in an environment where his speech might betray his identity. But reasonably speaking, Runo could only make for the Red Castle after tonight...

Well. His alleged helper must have found that key *somewhere*, indeed.

'Other question, then.' Another sip of beer. 'Why do you want her dead, your queen?'

'She's a murderer.'

'So you get another murderer to murder her in turn.' Runo grinned. 'Makes sense.'

'Look...' Again the masked stranger lost control of his voice for a moment. 'You're not here to ask these bloody questions, are you? You're here to accept my help and slit her throat. The Empress wrote you would follow my instructions without further hassle.'

'Ah, yes. She's quite an optimist, that Empress of mine.'

'She gave you *orders*.'

'She probably did, yes. She tends to give a lot of them.' Runo took his free hand off the chair's back and folded it around his glass without taking his eyes off the masked face in the shadows before him. 'But to tell you a little secret – I'm terrible at following instructions. I prefer not to ignore my own common sense, at least. Which the Empress knows, of course.'

'What are you trying to say?'

For the first time he detected a hint of doubt in the stranger's voice. Runo leaned back again, a little more leisurely than he felt. What was he trying to say? Even after a month of travelling, he wasn't sure himself. The Empress must have some reason to send *him* after this ridiculously promising opportunity, and he wasn't arrogant enough to believe she picked him because she liked him so much. Of course, he spoke the local language, but there were others who fulfilled that requirement. The Empress knew he tended to be a little more of a... loose projectile, too. So either she believed the job called for some more improvisation than her most slavish followers were capable of –

Or she found the entire situation as questionable as he did, and needed someone she wouldn't miss too much if things were to end unpleasantly.

In any case, it seemed she agreed with him that this wasn't work as usual. Not that *that* was much of a problem... Without thinking, he rubbed his fingers over the inner side of his left forearm, where his sleeve hid the row of short lines inked in his skin. But it quite suggested he should keep his eyes wide open for the days to come.

'One last thing,' he said, ignoring his conversation partner's question. 'Imagine any problems were to arise during my first explorations. Where do I find you?'

Again the man seemed hesitant for a moment. No, Runo concluded, he *very* much didn't want to be linked in any shape or form to the knife that would be found in his queen's chest within days.

'I'm around here every now and then,' the gruff voice said behind the mask. 'You can leave a letter for room twenty-four.'

'Lovely.' Runo finished his beer, picked up the rusty key from the table, and got to his feet. 'I'll get to work, then. Was a pleasure to meet you, brother.'

But the sense of unease lingered as he sauntered up the hill to the Red Castle the next morning, despite the crystal-clear forest air and the mild winter sun warming his back. He never got his missions mapped out for him this way, with a convenient traitor showing up to tell him exactly how to get into a castle unnoticed and how to break into his target's rooms. Not that it made sense to complain. Help was help...

But it meant he had to *rely* on someone.

This wasn't how he played the game, depending on the whims of others – this wasn't how he survived at the Taavi court. Don't get attached. It was the first rule of his world. Don't make friends you can't miss, don't save gold you can't bear to lose, don't hold principles you can't ignore. He knew the importance of that rule better than anyone else. Every single scheming nobleman that died under his knife violated it – clung too long to a friend fallen from grace, complained too much about the money he lost due to the Empress's decisions. The politics of home required flexibility, quick twists and turns. A flexibility he could do, normally.

But it was a damn lot harder to be intangible and untouchable if you were pinned into place by a plan someone else made for you.

Then again... He stepped aside to let a few wagons pass, then continued his walk. Even if he didn't like the look of it, what could he do? Take a few days off to investigate his mysterious accomplice first? He'd have to explain to the Empress why he had wasted so much time after his arrival in town, and she wouldn't be happy to hear he doubted her judgement. Already he could hear that deceptively girlish voice welcoming him back to Raulinna with all its razor-sharp sweetness – *You finished the job, yes, but isn't it a little curious it took you so much time just to confirm my simple instructions, Runo?*

Some impulsive decisions and unwanted creativity with her orders had already cost him a promotion to her elite corps of Silver Daggers twice, the rumours at court whispered. Not that he cared much about promotions, but her instructions were the one thing he should at least feel a little attached to. Fine, dying for the Taavi cause had never been his ambition, and he would be the last to sign up for a next military campaign into the unruly borderlands – but the Empress herself had saved his life, and he knew better than to betray her.

Which meant he wouldn't spend days digging into the background of his mysterious helper from room twenty-four. He'd just have to keep looking over his shoulder inside the Red Castle and hope his knife would keep him safe.

The building loomed over him as he walked on in his modest workman's clothes and threw smiles at all passers-by as if they should know his face. A multitude of mighty walls and towers, built from brick-red rocks contrasting starkly to the azure sky behind. In the late summer, when the forest turned that wine-red colour that had earned the kingdom its name, it would probably look like an extension of the foliage rather than like this imposing, impenetrable block of stone.

Runo's right hand wandered to the letter in his pocket, its wax seal a hard circle in the folds of the parchment. Really very, *very* convenient that someone had just handed him a ticket into the castle. Little chance the guards would let an unknown visitor pass, and the building didn't give the impression its inhabitants regularly forgot to lock the back door at night.

Again the discomfort stirred. A little too convenient to believe it, truly. Back home he would have recognised it as a trap without second thought – *nobody* at the Empress's court would ever be so helpful without a favour in return, and surely a man with access to Tamar's keys could think of easier ways to kill her. So what was the catch? He might as well get caught up in some double-edged plot to unmask the Empress's agents...

Then again, what was the use in unmasking an assassin who had been sitting in Raulinna until a month ago? Redwood should be focussing on unmasking the Taavi proxies already within their borders, not on importing more of them. He might as well use the letter, then – and in any case, what other options did he have?

So he pulled out the sealed parchment when he finally reached the castle's iron-plated gates, and handed it to the nearest guard with a nonchalant hand in his pocket and his most cheerful grin on his face. The guard gave him a glance of chronic suspicion as he broke the seal – admittedly not unjustly so – and read through the message while muttering sceptical remarks under his breath.

Then he read it again, now without the muttering.

He looked up, knitting his bushy eyebrows together, and examined Runo's face in silence for a few heartbeats. Runo smiled back at him. The guard looked back down, read the letter a third time, then cleared his throat and said, 'Ah.'

'I hope it's all clear?' Runo said breezily. Not that he knew what was supposed to be clear, but it couldn't hurt to make it sound a little more self-evident.

'Well.' The guard gave the letter a last glance, then pushed it back into Runo's hands, scowling like a man forced to hand over his hard-earned gold to a tax collector. Too attached to his pride, this fellow. 'I assume you know the way?'

'I do, thanks.'

The guard gestured him with obvious displeasure to walk on. Runo gave him a last grin, ambled through the high gates, and ran his eyes over the letter. A note from Queen Tamar herself, instructing the reader to let her contact through and not to speak about his arrival with a single living soul. Signed with the royal seal. Well. Looked like someone within the Red Castle was quite determined to give him a hand, indeed.

She's a murderer. Could that really be the full story, some revenge plot? But hiring someone else to execute your retaliation made no sense unless the kill came with too much of a risk to do it yourself.

Not the most pleasant of prospects.

Keeping his head low, Runo made a slow round through the ground floor of the castle, marking where he could find the dark corners to hide, the windows to climb from, the guards to look out for. The Red Castle was larger than he had expected from the ambassadors' tales – although still nowhere near the sprawling court at Raulinna. But the plastered walls with their green-and-gold paintings were charming enough, and when he glanced through an arrow-hole at the courtyard, the view over the surrounding woods was admittedly breathtaking.

Leaving the courtyard behind, he sauntered back inside, now following the directions of his masked accomplice. To the left, through the broad corridor that led along the northern wall. Half a floor up. To the right. The mass of people was thicker here, and less of them were servants – yes, his informant had mentioned that he should be approaching the castle's main hall now.

There it was, a wide-open door to his right. The crowd flocking around it seemed quite fixated on whatever went on inside, and by reflex Runo slowed down as he reached the broad archway. Look, he told the Empress in his thoughts, it would draw twice as much attention to walk on without paying attention – taking a look was his only sensible option. Couldn't hurt to know what was going on, could it?

He found a place behind a group of gawking young men near the doorway. There, hidden from most of the eyes inside, he fully turned to look.

Like the rest of the castle, the hall was larger than expected; the slender arches of the walls and ceiling came together so high above him that he had to lay his head in his neck to see them. The high, white walls were decorated with coats of arms and again those elegant paintings in moss green and gold. Sunlight fell in through the high windows to his right, spreading an unearthly amber glow over the hardwood floor.

A sight one could nearly call idyllic, if not for the scene taking place at the centre of the room.

A lonely man sat kneeling on the floorboards, his bald head shimmering with sweat, his voice too shrill as he loudly protested his arrest and the treatment he had received upon his arrival. Before him, on the stage at the far end of the hall, Runo's eyes finally found her –

Tamar. The Iron Queen of Redwood. The woman whose life he would end.

Looking nothing like the vague mental image he had carried along so far.

He had thought her to be around the Empress's age from the stories surrounding her name – nearing age fifty, although the Empress's hair dyes made good attempts to deny that fact. But Tamar looked no older than thirty, younger even than *he* was. Bright, copper-coloured hair, in tight braids around her head. A black widow's dress that made no efforts to hide the curves of her body underneath. A pale, heart-shaped face, lips set in hard lines, eyes cold and distant, a look demanding full and utter obedience from anyone laying eyes on her.

Runo let his breath escape in a long, slow hiss. She was a damn lot more beautiful than anticipated, admittedly, but at the sight of that expression it wasn't hard to imagine why even diplomats at the Empress's court spoke about her in a tone of palpable caution.

'... why I'm dragged before you like I'm some criminal or traitor!' the man kneeling on the floor continued, his shrill voice close to a shout. 'I'm entirely unaware of anything I did to deserve this treatment, and I—'

'Entirely unaware?' Her voice was a sea of rigid calm with perhaps a dash of indifference and amusement thrown in. 'That would make you stupid rather than innocent, Rusuvan. You must at least have some idea what I'd like to discuss with you.'

Words spoken like a fist in the face, with cool, calm self-assurance. The bald man kneeling before her had to hear that tone as well, had to hear the trap hidden below the words – but the poor bastard didn't give the impression he would withdraw anytime soon.

'Well...' An uncomfortable laugh. 'I suppose – if my niece's ridiculous accusations have reached the court as well...'

'Excellent,' Tamar said, folding her hands in her lap. 'Not stupid, then. In that case only the question of your innocence remains. Ridiculous, you said?'

'My niece – she seems to believe I was setting up some far-fetched plot to take the duchy from her hands? I suppose that fellow she married put the idea into her head – a Copper Coast exile, of all people! While I was spending a fortune on the best possible education in—'

'A fortune,' Tamar interrupted. 'The Tanglewood funds themselves, I suppose you mean?'

'Well – yes – I...'

"*Her* money, in other words.'

Another awkward laugh. 'Well, yes, but that doesn't make much of a difference, does it?'

'It makes the difference that you can hardly declare yourself some benevolent sponsor to her education,' Tamar said, waving his sentence away. 'But please continue. Did her education also require the hundreds of additional silver pieces that mysteriously disappeared from the duchy's administration while she was staying abroad?'

A thorny silence fell. Tamar sat straight up in her seat, her face a mask of cool amusement – the face of a woman who knew exactly how much she was on the winning side, and didn't have the patience to be subtle about it. None of the treacherous sweetness the Empress employed in these situations, the honeyed sympathy that could turn deadly in the blink of an eye, that suspicious kindness that could still end with a dozen guards dragging you from your bed the next morning. Just simple, straight-forward bluntness, and somehow that sent the hairs in Runo's neck rising all the same.

'And I suppose you were so disappointed about her untimely return from her educational travels,' Tamar continued, sounding nearly bored, 'that you subsequently decided to never speak or meet with a single civilised person in Redwood again? That instead you would quietly spend your days in a mansion just over the Androughan border, far away from me and my guards?'

She looked so damn unmovable, stable enough to rival the hill her castle was built on. Around him, the first muffled murmurs rose from the gathered audience, whispered speculations and accusations...

'Silence,' Tamar said, without raising her voice.

And in the blink of an eye the hall went eerily quiet again, silent enough to hear the heavy breathing of the man kneeling in the middle.

Runo nearly laughed. *She's a murderer.* He knew the kind – just another noble with tyrannical tendencies, one of the many who got drunk on their power and ended up believing that every little nuisance they encountered was a disgraceful attack on nature itself. Just the type that flocked to the Taavi court like flies to honey. Sooner or later they always made the same mistake, overestimated their own brilliance and made just one enemy too many. Was that what had happened? Had she grown a little too attached to the rush of her own power, sentenced one man too many, misjudged the grudges of her court?

'Your Majesty...' the kneeling man began. At her hardwood throne, Tamar sighed.

'If that's all you have to say for now, Rusuvan, you're free to go. Don't leave the Red Castle. My judges will look into the matter over the following days.' A quick smile. 'Of course, being an innocent man, you have no reason to go anywhere else until you have proven your innocence.'

'But Your Majesty—'

'You can go.'

Judges. Runo nearly scoffed as the bald man clambered to his feet and the crowd shrunk away around him. Was there even the smallest chance those judges would end up declaring their suspect innocent? They had likely been instructed already, the verdict already written; a woman taking her own crown that seriously would never risk being humiliated by an acquittal in public. He should know. His first official target had been the Novaini governor who bribed the jury to his side in a court case between himself and one of the Empress's puppets. Somehow people never understood that fighting was useless when their opponent wore a crown.

Then again, the unlucky Rusuvan might actually get out of his predicament if this mission continued to progress as swiftly as it had so far.

Runo shook his head as he sauntered on, the image of Tamar still bright on his mind's eye. Up the stairs, through the corridor his masked friend described to him last night. His earlier cautiousness moved over for simple resolve mixed with a hint of impatience, the feeling of a mission he ought to finish soon. They got on his nerves, her type of people, irked him in a way he could feel itching under his skin. They took themselves so bloody seriously, were so unhealthily convinced of their own invulnerability. The Empress, of course, was worst of all, and if he hadn't owed her his life, he might well have left the court a long time ago. But from the first glimpse of her, Tamar made good efforts to rise to similar levels of unpleasantness.

Without thought he rubbed his fingers over the inside of his arm. Forty-two lines. Soon there would be forty-three of them.

Left before the next staircase, around a weathered wooden statue, and there it was – the door marked with an ancient Redwood rune. For a moment he listened sharply. No footsteps approaching. With a quick movement he pulled the rusty key from his pocket and stuck it into the lock. The mechanism turned without a sound.

He slipped into the empty, dusty bedroom and closed the door behind him again, unable to suppress his grin.

From here on it should be an easy job. Three more deserted rooms, all connected, and in the last he would find the door to Tamar's own bedroom, the lock of which he could open with this same key. A quick kill, an easy way out, and by the time her guards would find her tomorrow, he would be long gone from the castle. Now he only had to amuse himself for a few hours in these unused bedrooms. He might as well take a nap until it was time for work.

Unusually comfortable for a mission. Perhaps he should have been a little more grateful to his masked helper last night. The man surely *had* done his best to wipe his queen from the face of the earth.

There was a wry kind of justice to it, Runo considered as he fell down on the nearest bed – for her to be betrayed by one of her own rather than by outside mingling. In the end it always happened, didn't it? If they just pushed hard enough, eventually even the unbeatable were beaten, the indestructible destroyed. As they should be. He probably shouldn't feel so satisfied at the thought alone, but Tamar's face still lingered before him when he closed his eyes – hard, unrelenting, stability to the point of becoming overconfidence –

He didn't even want to hurt her. He just wanted to bring her off balance. To disrupt that well-behaved existence she'd arranged around herself, to defy her expectations for once – to throw her world upside down, wipe that imperturbable look from her annoyingly beautiful face, and tell her, now who's in charge here?

In all likeliness, a knife through her heart would quite get that point across.

CHAPTER 2

The door of her bedroom fell shut behind Tamar, silencing the unbearable murmur of voices outside and forcing a far more unbearable silence upon her buzzing mind.

A quick glance through the room confirmed no one was waiting for her inside – not Amiran, not Lasha, not one of the useless men she'd allowed into her room over the last months. Only after she checked and double-checked that she was alone did she curse and sag down on the edge of her bed, burying her face in her hands. It didn't suppress the thoughts crawling up on her, creeping into her room from the cracks and corners.

Damn Rusuvan, denying all guilt despite the financial chaos that had swept over his duchy in the years he ruled it in his niece's name. Damn his friends, too, besieging her with their requests and objections... *Surely* it couldn't be as bad as one hysterical girl made it sound, they insisted. Was she really going to trust a young lass silly enough to marry a Copper Coast exile without even a thought at the political consequences?

Damn her brother-in-law most of all, who had smugly suggested giving the man a Lord's Trial, allowing the other nobles of the kingdom to judge him. They both knew Rusuvan's old friends would absolve him without even taking the evidence into account. An outcome that would send all deceitful lords throughout the kingdom the crystal-clear message that fraud was now an offence you could easily get away with.

Tomorrow her story had to be clear. Tomorrow she had to know what to say and what not to say, who to threaten, who to ignore, who to flatter – how to tell the world that the shifty bastard would still explain himself to a selected group of judges with no reason to favour him. But one night was woefully short to make a plan...

With a muffled groan she stood up, let down her hair, then took the small knife from the pocket hidden in her skirt and shoved it underneath her pillow. She was tempted, very tempted to simply tell all troublemakers they could either shut up or see their head end up on a pole. But some of the bastards provided their own soldiers, and putting heads on poles had become a little more complicated since Anzor was no longer around to guarantee the loyalty of half of her army.

She scoffed and glanced at the burn scars on her arms as she stripped off her dress. Damn Anzor, too. Perhaps a scoop of belladonna in a few glasses at the breakfast table would also solve this problem.

Then again – people remembered Anzor's death. Better not to give them the slightest reason to believe she was responsible for that poison in her husband's wine.

She sighed, swung her black dress over the chair beside her bed, and pulled her peignoir from the closet. Murder wouldn't be the answer in this case. No, she'd ask Zovinar to publicly request a common trial for her uncle. As a last resort she could always write some foreign noblemen who clashed with Rusuvan over the years and tell the court she had to choose a common trial to soothe international tensions.

She sank down in the chair at her desk and pulled a new sheet of parchment from the upper drawer. No time to lose, then. *Dear Zovinar...*

Behind her, a metallic click broke the pressing silence.

Tamar froze, her pen dripping ink above the parchment. Was that the lock behind her? No, that was impossible – the only key was hers. Only a handful of people even knew that way in existed, and she made clear to all of them that spreading the secret would have unpleasant consequences. It was doubtlessly something else, something sounding accidentally similar – just a sword of her guards ticking against the wall outside, or...

Another sound interrupted her thoughts, the scraping of a doorhandle turning down.

A creak of the hinges.

A footstep.

And silence again – dead and utter silence, as if she had imagined every single sound behind her back.

Only then did she regain her senses, in an explosion of alarm that sent her heart pounding into her throat. With a brusque, uncontrolled movement she dropped her pen and jerked around in her chair. There, in the doorway that had been locked until moments ago –

A man.

A man whose face she'd never seen before, dark curls and a nose that had been broken at least once, a hint of a careless smile around his lips. Southern, his olive skin suggested. Simple workman's clothes – but his shirt didn't conceal the shape of his muscular arms, a build that suggested he was more familiar with a sword than with a plough. His one hand rested on the doorhandle, the key sticking from the lock below. In the other hand –

Gleaming strangely blueish in the candlelight, a knife.

It took her perplexed mind a moment too long – a man, with a knife. In her bedroom. Smiling that strangely cheerful smile at her. Looking about as southern as the Taavi Empress herself.

The Empress.

Good gods.

Getting killed was the only thing that could make this night even worse.

And at once her mind functioned again, the thought of murder spinning it back into motion. Hell's sake, she wasn't going to *die* on this unremarkable winter evening, was she? She wasn't going to let Rusuvan out that easily. Thoughts burst through her in less than the time it took to blink an eye – the guards outside her room? The assassin stood too close to the path between her desk and the door. Could she scream? The door held all sound – she had *ordered* it to hold all sound. Her own knife? Under her pillow already, and her bed stood a good ten feet away.

Another reflex kicked in. Show no weakness. Show no hesitation. If she wanted to get out of whatever this situation was, she couldn't afford to lose control of it for even a moment.

'Well.' At least she sounded quite convincingly like herself. 'Good evening?'

'Evening,' he said – in her own language. Why did he speak her language? His voice was a deep baritone, the accent just a little different from the usual Taavi accent – but what exactly the difference was Tamar couldn't tell, and couldn't be bothered to think about. 'Quite late to still be working, isn't it?'

'Could say the same to you,' she said, glancing at the knife again in spite of herself. Show no weakness – but the blue gleam of the metal made the blood in her veins run cold. Three steps forward and he would be close enough to stab the blade into her chest. 'To what do I owe the visit?'

The Taavi stepped aside, shut the door behind him, and leaned back against the wall. He carried himself with an insufferable nonchalance – as if he were truly just paying her a complimentary visit. As if he would happily accept a glass of wine, bring a toast to her health, and walk off again. As if he weren't holding that knife at all.

'I'm afraid you annoyed my Empress a little too much.'

The bloody Empress, indeed. It took all she had not to close her eyes and curse. What had she done? Made too much of an effort to keep the Five Kingdoms together despite the conflicts of the past years? Cooperated too smoothly with Viviette and the Androughan warlords to keep the dragons in the mountains safe from the interest of the Empire?

Did it matter?

Tamar sucked in a breath and forced the skin of her throat to forget that imagined touch of razor-sharp iron. She couldn't die. Not now. Not tonight. Redwood needed her to survive. But the assassin would know better than to let her reach the door, and her only other hope at survival lay underneath a pillow on the other side of the room.

'Quite unfortunate,' she said. Keep control, her thoughts were repeating, like a nauseating little nursery song. Don't show weakness. Ignore that pounding heart. Keep control. 'I've never been assassinated before. How do these things come about? Am I allowed any last wishes, or do you just slit my throat and disappear into the night again?'

Amusement flickered in his eyes. 'Depending on what the last wish is, I may allow you one. Not really according to protocol, I will admit, but I tend to be relatively accommodating with these things.'

Accommodating. The Taavi Empress had sent an *accommodating* assassin into her bedroom. With a joyless laugh she said, 'I can't believe my luck.'

'Oh, you could have gotten way worse.' He gave her a fake-modest grin, ignoring the sarcasm. 'So, any requests? Something to drink? A last prayer?'

Tamar closed her eyes, thoughts flashing by at lightning speed. Keep control. Her knife – she had to get to her knife. But what could she tell him? I'd like to die in my own familiar bed, comfortably close to that specific green pillow over there? If the bastard had somehow gotten his hands on the key to her bedroom, he wouldn't be stupid. He had to suspect that she wouldn't give up so easily. If he was thinking straight he'd refuse any request more suspicious than that suggested last drink...

How did you make a murderer think a little less straight?

She opened her eyes again, a resigned determination hardening inside her. The Taavi was still smiling at her, golden-eyed and broad-shouldered, his handsome face contrasting sharply with the ugly gleam of the knife between his fingers.

Well.

She could have gotten worse, indeed.

Holding his gaze, she turned towards him in her chair and crossed her legs. Her trembling fingers blindly found the knot of the silk sash around her waist. For the first time a hint of surprise rose in the assassin's eyes – although he recovered so quickly she nearly missed it.

'Ah,' he said dryly. 'A new strategy. Hoping I'll be so dazzled by your alluring appearance that I forget about my job?'

No, he wasn't stupid. Then again, if he wanted alluring – he could get alluring.

'I wouldn't complain if you forgot.' The silk of her peignoir fell open, although hindered by the back of the chair and her legs; he wouldn't see more than the skin between her breasts, her belly, her thighs hiding the last secrets of her body. 'But I didn't count on it, to be honest.'

His quick glance over her nakedness didn't escape her. Nonchalance or not – he knew exactly what she offered him, and it certainly didn't leave him indifferent.

'So what are you hoping I'll do?'

'If I can be honest anyway...' Tamar shrugged, and the silk slid another inch over her shoulders. She barely suppressed a shiver, fear as much as the cold air on her skin. 'My husband died a good year ago. It's been lonely enough since, and I'd hate to die that way. You'd do me a favour by lifting the loneliness a little.'

He slowly, very slowly, tilted his head. This time his gaze running over her was nowhere near quick or subtle. Good gods, he *wasn't* ugly, despite that slightly crooked nose and the skewed smile around his lips – which should be a relief with the lengths she was prepared to go to survive, and felt strangely dangerous at the same time.

'I see,' he said.

Something about the tone of his voice made the hairs in the back of her neck stand up. A mixture of thoughtfulness and amusement and something nearly like a challenge.

'I'm glad to hear.' Keep control. 'So – how accommodating will you be?'

Again that look darting over her skin. Then he said, 'Stand up.'

When had she last taken orders – *anyone's* orders? But he still held that knife...

The silk of her peignoir fell along her body as she stood up, drawing his eyes to her half-bared breasts again. For a moment neither of them moved, a moment like the silence before a judge's verdict was spoken. Every inch of her skin prickled under his gaze. If he refused to touch her, if he would dutifully finish his job – she was a dead woman. If he accepted the invitation...

She'd have to stand his hands on her. But she *might* live.

'Step closer.'

Something in his voice made it so infuriatingly easy to obey his commands – a polished, melodious undertone of authority, cutting through even the rush of her fear. She stepped closer. At the wall, a mere stride away from her, the assassin smiled.

'Don't like following orders, do you?'

'You're holding a knife,' she managed with something like a laugh. 'That would take the joy of obedience from everyone, I'd say.'

He glanced down at the weapon. 'And yet I'm supposed to believe you'll happily throw yourself into my arms?'

Tamar didn't dare to breathe. Not showing fear was much easier if she simply didn't show anything at all.

'Still hoping for me to lose my mind, aren't you?' he continued slowly, his voice amused as much as threatening. 'All murderers must be brainless savages, after all. But being fucked by a brainless savage could just be worth it if I then forget to draw my knife in a burst of passion...'

She closed her eyes. The assassin sniggered.

'I doubt I'll forget. But if that doesn't discourage you, feel free to try me.'

When she looked up, he'd just slipped the knife back into some sheath hidden in the pocket of his trousers. A meagre comfort – he was half a head taller, his shoulders twice as broad as hers. Even without his knife he would easily overpower her in a physical struggle, and his calm confidence suggested he knew it as well as she did. But at least he wouldn't take her with a blade to the throat.

At least he didn't suspect anything about the weapon under her pillow.

She took a deep breath, suppressed a shiver. Well, damn it. Whatever he'd do to her, it could hardly be worse than dying.

'Show me some brainless savagery, then, Taavi.'

A grin spread over his face, mockery rather than triumph. 'I'm very sorry, Your Majesty. I'm terrible at following instructions.'

'What...'

Now finally he moved away from the wall, a single step, ending up half an arm's length away from her. Her voice failed her, and once again he smiled, raising his hands to her shoulders. Only with the greatest of efforts did she manage not to flinch – but his fingers found her skin with startling gentleness, none of the violent greed she expected, none of Pridon's disregard, none of Anzor's roughness. Soft, deliberate touches, fingers caressing the lines of her collarbone like musician's fingers dancing over an instrument.

Her breath caught in her throat. Drowned out by the rush of her racing heartbeat, the assassin chuckled and brushed her peignoir off her shoulders.

The silk slid away like it was glad to let go. Yet he did not hold still, skimming his hands over her body, exploring her with a purposeful intensity as if every thought in his mind was focussed on the tiny surface where his fingertips met her skin. For a moment his touch lingered at the burn scars on her upper arms, but he moved on without speaking. Past her elbows, playing along her lower arms in slow, spiralling circles. Over her hips and up along her sides again, until his warm hands lay around her waist – to constrain her or to catch her if her knees gave in, she couldn't tell. His smell drifted around her, a southern scent of sweet spices, cloves, and cinnamon. Even with her eyes closed she felt the nearness of his strong body, the warmth emanating off him, his gaze branding her skin.

For a fraction of a moment she no longer knew what her plan was.

'Well, Your Majesty?' he muttered, and the undeniable mockery in his voice shook her back awake. 'Any other requests?'

'My bed.' Her voice came out too hoarse. Arousal stirred in her guts, deadly and desperate; under those persuasive hands, not even the thought of the knife in his pocket seemed so urgent anymore. For hell's sake – what was she *thinking*? He would kill her – he would *kill* her – and she had a kingdom to take care of – people to protect, wars to prevent –

'Your bed?' He chuckled. 'A little boring, wouldn't you say?'

Her heart skipped a beat. 'What?'

He moved forward, pushing her back, and not towards her bed at all – past her desk, until she felt the cold wall against her naked back and could move no further, caught between his scorching body and the cold stones. Pressed against him, she could feel the hard ridges of his muscles below the homespun cloth – muscles trained to kill her, but there was no bloodlust in the way he trailed his lips along her neck, then nuzzled her earlobe.

'I could take you here,' he said softly, and in that strange, golden voice, it didn't sound like a threat at all. Here. Back against the wall, in his muscular arms. Oh, gods. 'Could have you right against this wall. Would you like that, Your Majesty?'

She struggled for breath, and for sensible thoughts. Yes. No. Yes, hell knew she would – but the wall didn't offer her any knives, and she *wouldn't* enjoy dying...

'Not what I had in mind,' she managed, and again he laughed.

'A shame. Then how about...'

He spun her around in his arms and swung her over her own desk, allowing her to catch her weight on her elbows just before her full torso was pressed against the smooth wood. She was too surprised to cry out, too surprised to struggle. People didn't fling her over desks, for hell's sake. People did *not* fling her over desks. But the assassin held her down so easily, his hand on her shoulder the most careful vice in the world – there's no use to struggling, that hand said, but don't worry, I won't give you a reason to struggle either... Standing behind her, he clawed his other hand into her exposed bottom, and to her own mortification she nearly moaned.

'Or here?' he suggested, shameless amusement in his voice. A cat playing with its prey – and yet he didn't hurt her. Why didn't he hurt her? Was he taking pleasure in her confusion, his uncontested power? 'Any opinions, Your Majesty?'

Tamar squeezed her eyes shut, desperately trying not to make a sound as he trailed his fingers over the curves of her body. His touch numbed every anxious thought, the diplomatic worries and the political game, until even the fear was nothing but a faint discordant tone in the back of her brain – her knife, the last spark of sense whispered, she had to get to her knife... But how would she move with those confident fingers kneading her body?

'No?' His hands disappeared from her sides when she stayed silent, leaving cold, lonely skin behind. 'Highly unfortunate. We'll have to go with boring, then.'

He lifted her before she understood what was happening, effortlessly as if she were still the spindly girl she'd been at sixteen years old. Boring. Was this *boring*, the strangely tender, unmistakably commanding way he laid her down in the soft wool of her blankets? He massaged her shoulders, then slid his hands along the lines of her body, stroking the onset of her breasts with his thumbs at their passing. Her sides. Her hips. Touches so purposeful they were nearly reassuring... Tamar clenched her teeth, battling the resignation washing over her, the ridiculous desire to just *give in*. The blankets seemed to smother her, and so did the sensation of his brazen fingers digging into her skin, the smell of the fire, and the rich, intoxicating fragrance of his body. She had to fight. She *had* to fight. But to fight she'd have to break free from the command of his hands, from the tempting certainty of his control that took the heavy responsibility from her mind and offered her this blameless bliss instead...

The assassin's fingers dug into the hungry flesh of her thighs to spread them, and the flames of her desire burst out into a flaring bonfire – oh, gods. Keep control, Tamar. Keep *control*. She had to concentrate. His breathtaking caresses didn't matter, and neither did the agonising hunger aching between her legs, the painfully pleasurable idea of this man inside her – she had to *survive*. Her knife. The pillow. Just out of reach, but if she could get a fraction closer –

He sat leaning over her when she opened her eyes, supporting himself with one knee on the edge of her mattress, a faint smile as their gazes met.

'Yes,' he said softly. 'You have been lonely for a very long time, haven't you?'

Tamar came up and grabbed him by the front of his shirt, rolling him over in her blankets. Her limbs acted in a rush of reflexes, shocked awake from the passive haze of her lust – her knees pinned him into place with all her weight, her hand slapped the pillow aside and snatched the knife from the silk. Then the blade lay against his throat, trembling along with her fingers, but reassuringly heavy.

Underneath the weapon, the assassin froze.

'Don't move.' Damn the hoarseness in her voice – damn her body remembering the feel of his fingers. 'If you move...'

She sucked in a breath. Her heart hammered so violently that it made her light-headed. If you move, she wanted to say, I'll kill you. I've killed before. Don't think I'll hesitate. But he smiled at her, a smile that made her remember with painful sharpness how naked she was, how close he was, how warm and hard underneath her, and the words froze on her lips.

'If I move?' he repeated. Knife against his throat or not, he sounded amused.

'Put your hands over your head,' she managed, and his smile broadened to a grin.

'That will require some movement, I'm afraid.'

Already the control was slipping from her hands – she could feel it seeping through her fingers, mirrored in the mocking gleam in his eyes. What did she think she was doing – naked, straddling a Taavi assassin, pressing a knife she didn't dare to use against his throat?

'Move, then,' she said. 'But slowly.'

At least he followed that command. Tamar took her free hand from his chest and moved it to his hip, fumbling along the hard lines of his body by touch alone – a body that could have been hers if only she'd been prepared to die for it... She found the cold metal of his knife against his thigh at her first try. Without taking her eyes from his she pulled the weapon from his pocket and threw it into the room, out of reach for both of them. It clattered against the wall as if to sound the alarm. No reaction from the guards outside followed.

Only one option left, then.

For a last moment she held his gaze – golden eyes gleaming with a mixture of lust and mockery and vigilant sharpness. Then she jumped, lurched away from him before he could move, and dashed to the other side of the room with all the panic-induced speed her muscles could deliver. The door – the *door*.

He jumped up as soon as her knife disappeared from his throat. He was too late.

With a feeling of dizzying triumph she swung open her bedroom door. The castle's noise streamed into the room again, a noise she had never loved so much – and then the alarmed cries of her guards, the shrieks of metal, the cold air from the corridors reaching her burning, naked skin –

And the assassin, stumbling to a halt in the middle of her room, his mouth half-opened to shout, his eyes staring at her with wild, thinly veiled disbelief.

She wanted to laugh. Wanted to tell him that of course she wouldn't throw herself into some murderer's arms – but the desire was still burning its blazing path through her, and the words didn't find her lips. Around her, her men stormed into the room. Someone threw her peignoir over her shoulders. Outside a voice shouted for reinforcements. Suddenly it took all she had not to sink through her knees and crawl up in some dark corner like a little child fleeing her nightmares. But her guards were still here to see her – the *assassin* was still here to see her –

Although he was busier shrinking back from her men at this moment, his vigilant eyes focussed on the young guard closing in on him with a drawn sword. Ready to kill. Which was exactly the order she should give...

Except that the key was still sticking in the lock behind her.

Oh, gods be damned.

'Keep him alive,' she snapped, her voice too hoarse. 'Gocha, get back – he's unarmed. Arrest him, put him in a cell. Alive. Understood?'

The young guard faltered and stepped back, his sword still in position for attack. As always he avoided her gaze when he turned towards her, blinking at the floor around her feet instead. 'Your Majesty – he tried to *kill* you!'

'Yes, and I doubt he did it alone.' Where had he found that key? How had he even sneaked into the castle? 'Get him out of my sight. I want a word with him tomorrow.'

Gocha lowered his sword half an inch, although clearly unwillingly. Only now, with his back against the wall, did the assassin look up to meet her gaze again – a sharp, calculating look that emphatically ignored her naked body and set every inch of her aflame nonetheless.

'Much appreciated,' he said.

But she heard the challenge in his tense voice. You haven't won, that undertone told her – the game isn't over yet. We've barely just began.

CHAPTER 3

Someone had died in these dungeons.

It was the first impression that fully hit Runo's senses as the young guard threw him into the cold cell and shut the barred door behind him – the faint but all too familiar stench of rotting flesh, so sweet that his nostrils seemed to curl inward at the first whiff. It was that smell of death and decay that blocked his common sense for a moment too long as he sat kneeling in the hay and sand and tried not to gag. By the time he dragged his thoughts away from the lurking memories in the depths of his mind, Tamar's guards had already walked off into the darkness, leaving him alone with the icy cellar air and the rustling of rats in the distance.

Well.

This was all less than ideal.

He got back to his feet, groaning, cursing the useless arousal still twisting through his veins, the half-hard erection that hadn't yet realised how far Tamar's luscious body was removed from him now. By touch he found something like a bed in the darkness, little more than a broad shelf with a thin layer of linen. Below it lay a tattered woollen blanket. Better than nothing. He sank down onto the creaking wood and closed his eyes, again breathing in the old smell of death. The memory of white, dead faces returned to his mind's eye with unsettling ease, staring at him from over their unfinished dinner table.

'I know,' Runo muttered. 'Might join you soon.'

In this ratty cell, it was nearly a reassuring thought. At least there was one company that would never disappear on him.

He fumbled the blanket around his shoulders and leaned back against the rough stone wall, wrapping his arms around himself to suppress the cold shivers. With the shock waning, his thoughts slowly adjusted to this new reality – a state of affairs that saw him locked up deep under the Red Castle, unarmed and vulnerable, while his supposed victim was still walking around above him. Gods be damned. He should have known it could never be so easy. He should have known not to underestimate bloody Tamar with her bloody last wishes – should have known better than to let his mind run off with the unexpected temptation of her nakedness.

He shivered again, and this time it wasn't the cold alone. The memory of that voluptuous body pressed against his chest still lingered on his skin.

In hindsight it was all utterly ridiculous. What had he thought – that a woman confronted with her own near death would happily throw himself into her murderer's arms? But he'd seen that stone-hard resolution melt from her face, heard the hoarseness of her voice in those two words – *my bed.* He'd seen how she moved towards his touches – how her eyes gleamed at him the moment before she caught him by surprise with that knife against his throat.

Perhaps he had been overly enthusiastic to believe her, yes. At least he wouldn't have taken that impulsive decision if she hadn't been so dreadfully beautiful, without her stiff braids and that cold black dress. But if she'd been acting, her performance was to blame as much as his own stupidity, and the alternative...

It's been lonely enough since.

He shook his head so violently he nearly slammed his own skull into the wall. Hell's sake, he should stop thinking about Tamar and her vexingly soft skin. Her bloody loneliness, real or not, was the last of his troubles. Had he forgotten the merciless edge in her voice that afternoon, the stench of decay in her cells? She wasn't the type to show mercy on an enemy assassin she had no use for. *I want a word with him tomorrow*, yes, but what would she do after that word?

Runo buried his face in his hands. She needed his information, of course. She'd want to know who helped him to devise his attempt at her life – not that he knew – and she might be quite desperate for that knowledge, too. So if he didn't tell her, she probably wouldn't kill him at once. Then again, being tortured wasn't a great alternative, and either way she would give up on him sooner or later if he kept his mouth shut for too long.

The smell of rotting meat crowded thicker and thicker around him, as if the dead body still lay in the next cell, attracting flies and sniffling rats. For hell's sake, he had to keep his head clear. This was not the moment to get lost in the memories of Sidra. He should stay alive first. How did you convince a queen not to kill her enemy's assassin?

What did Tamar want?

He muttered a curse. He probably knew a rumour or two about the Empress's court she'd like to hear – but there was little sense in escaping the Red Castle if he would subsequently be skinned alive at his return to Raulinna. Coming home while Tamar was still walking and breathing would be dangerous enough in itself... Already he could hear that sweet voice speaking down at him from the throne in the Glass Hall. *If I send you after a promising opportunity to remove one of my most troublesome adversaries, Runo, I don't expect you to fuck her first thing after your arrival and then let her escape.*

Runo grimaced. No, bad idea. If he wanted to come out of this entire damn mission alive, he should get out of his cell, kill Tamar anyway, and pray the Empress would be so kind to gloss over the unusual end to his first attempt. But he didn't even know how he would escape in the first place, let alone kill her.

What did she want?

Not to be lonely.

He let out a joyless chuckle. Utter madness, of course – but the idea clicked into place in his thoughts and didn't let go again. If she hadn't been acting...

Outside his cell, breaking through the deep silence of the darkness, a door creaked.

Runo froze on his meagre bed. The dungeons were silent again, but he was pretty damn sure he had heard the sound – someone passing the thick iron door separating the dungeons from the more inhabitable parts of the Red Castle. A guard coming to check on him? But hardly an hour had gone by since they dropped him off, and as far as he had seen on his way down, that single door was the only exit. They might as well just stay up there, where the air was warmer, and didn't stink of death. And even *if* someone was coming this way to see if he was still where he ought to be, that person should at least have brought a lantern. Not the faintest trace of a flame lit the darkness outside the barred door of his cell, though.

He sat perked up, listening sharply. No, he wasn't going mad; silent footsteps were coming closer indeed. Another sound, too, with irregular intervals – wood scraping along the rough stone walls? Then the footsteps held still, and only a slight screak still broke the silence.

Then –

The twinge of a string snapping back in place and a hissed curse of pain.

Runo's breath caught in his throat. He knew that sound, had heard it perhaps a hundred times while the Empress's soldiers were training around him – accompanied by similar curses, too, whenever the novices made a mistake. A crossbow. Someone was trying to cock a bloody *crossbow* mere yards away from his cell, and not to pass by for a pleasant chat and a cup of tea, presumably.

I want a word with him tomorrow.

It took an effort not to curse. He didn't even know who helped him, and yet everybody was planning to kill him over it in this place?

Already the footsteps were moving again, coming closer far, far faster than his panicking mind could think. Cover. He needed cover, but this barred door was about as useful as an open doorway, and a ratty blanket wouldn't help him much either...

His bed.

Or what went for a bed, at least.

In one supple movement he ducked underneath the wooden board, pulling up his legs to stay out of an arrow's path. In the darkness he couldn't say if he was out of reach entirely, but he'd rather take an arrow in the foot than one in the heart.

The footsteps came to a halt, close enough to hear his visitor's quiet breathing. Runo lay frozen. Perhaps, some ridiculously optimistic part of his mind suggested, the man would just turn around and leave if it looked like he wasn't here after all? Then his sensible thoughts kicked in. If he was unlucky, the unknown other would return with a torch to see whether he was still in his cell, and then there would be no hiding in the darkness anymore.

In a flash of inspiration, he made a soft, murmuring sound, like a dreaming man talking in his sleep. Two snoring breaths. Silence again for a few heartbeats, then another few snores. How did he even sound while he slept? Perhaps he should snore a little louder, just to make the point?

But the arrow slammed into the wood above his head before he could spend another thought on his acting.

Time to wake up, then. Tugging at the bed to make the wood creak a little, Runo made some groaning sounds and grumbled, 'What in the world...'

The near inaudible click of the crossbow cocking again. Runo's mind was working at top speed now – the more arrows his attacker would fire, the higher the chance one of them *would* actually hit its target. The next one had to hit the mark. Although it probably shouldn't kill him at once – that would be *too* much of a lucky strike.

A short whizz, another weight slamming into the wood just above his head. Runo screamed, in his best imitation of the knight he'd seen taking an arrow in the knee once – shrill curses intermixed with furious, panted questions as to what in the damned world was happening, and was the bastard trying to kill him, or what? Make enough noise, his mind pressed, enough to hide the fact that the next arrow won't sound like it's burying itself into human flesh at all...

Another whistling sound, another whack, and he abruptly let his screams die away. Some hoarse panting, a rasping, choking cough, a last groan.

Then silence – breathless, frightened silence.

He didn't hear his attacker move for at least a minute. Then, when he remained silent, the swish of a cloak in the darkness, the thudding of footsteps disappearing in the distance again. Still Runo didn't dare to move. Only when he heard the iron door open and fall shut again did he cautiously slip his hand around the wooden board and grabble along the linen-covered surface. He found the arrows nearly at once, sticking into the wood mere inches from where his head would have lain if he had indeed been sleeping.

Cold sweat trickled along his back as he sat up and sucked in a deep breath, savouring the sensation of the air in his living lungs. His limbs started shaking, and he couldn't bring them to stop; the world around him shrank to the agonising cold running up his veins, the stench of rot curling through his nostrils, the heart still pounding in his chest. Empty eyes staring at him from all sides, ready to welcome them in their middle. Hell be damned. He wasn't going to sleep tonight. He might never sleep again.

But at least...

He rested his head against the cold wall and managed a joyless chuckle into nothingness. At least he'd have something to say to Tamar tomorrow morning.

CHAPTER 4

Amiran burst into her room three minutes after the blaring trumpets outside signalled the change of guards – his shirt not even buttoned yet, his hands blotted with graphite stains. He was still clutching a wooden folding rule. Abruptly pulled away from his research – not something that happened easily.

'What in the damn world – someone tried to *kill* you?'

'Morning, Amiran,' Tamar said, looking up from her half-finished letter to Tanglewood and forcing the corners of her mouth into a calm, composed smile she didn't feel. The curious glances of her guards outside the door were painful stings in the edges of her sight; she could only guess how many more people were listening along out of sight, eager for the next piece of juicy gossip, the slightest sign of weakness. 'I received an unexpected visitor, yes. Mind closing the door?'

'An unexpected *visitor*?' His voice soared up. 'Why didn't you wake me, for hell's sake? If I'd known—'

'Amiran, the *door*.'

Her cousin froze three steps into her room, moved a step back and slammed the door shut. In the same furious tone he continued, 'What for the gods' sake happened?'

Tamar closed her eyes for a heartbeat. 'The Empress sent an assassin into my bedroom.'

'I heard that much, thank you. Details?'

For a moment too long she was silent, lost for words under his piercing look. Details. What was she supposed to say? A man with an infuriating smile stepped into my room and took possession of me until even dying didn't seem such a bad option after all. Then I didn't die. What would he *think* of her if he knew how her body had betrayed her under the assassin's hands?

'I kept him talking for a while,' she said.

The words came over her lips as if she were discussing some tedious meeting with the tax department, calm to the point of sounding bored. As if she hadn't lain awake for a full night, trying to shake off the memory of those insistent fingers on her skin.

'You *talked*.' The scepticism in his voice was painfully obvious.

'He was surprisingly accommodating,' Tamar said. She shouldn't have. A decidedly unwelcome warmth flickered through her at the word alone. 'And he didn't expect me to have a knife. I was lucky enough to surprise him and warn the guards in time.'

'The guards,' Amiran said, falling down on the edge of her bed and throwing his ruler aside, 'said something along the lines of you being naked.'

She stared at him, or perhaps rather at the bed behind him, that bed where the Taavi had lowered her into the blankets with such ease and laid claim onto her body like it belonged to him. Gods be damned, what had the bastard done to her? At the thought alone she could feel his fingers squeezing her inner thighs again, opening her up for him with a touch that, no matter how tender, left no room for objections. Naked, yes, in a way she hadn't been naked for a long time –

'I was going to bed,' she said, averting her eyes to force the memories from her mind's eye. She had to be calm. She had to be determined. She had to be a queen of iron, or at least pretend to be a queen of iron as long as she needed to convince the rest of the world that sending murderers after her wouldn't achieve much. 'I hadn't taken the possibility of assassins into account when I undressed.'

Amiran bit out a curse. 'Did he touch you?'

'Barely.'

'Tamar...'

'Oh, please.' Too curt. Too quick. But she couldn't bear to speak of it, the fire he had kindled under her skin – because it still smouldered there, far too close to the surface, and she couldn't, *couldn't* allow it to flare up again. 'My unblemished virtue doesn't really seem the first of our problems, does it?'

'He did touch you, then?'

'Barely, I said.'

'For the bloody gods' sake, I—'

'Leave it *be*, Amiran. It's of no importance.'

He sucked in a sharp breath, but swallowed his obvious frustration. 'Then what is the first of our problems, you'd say?'

'He found a way in,' Tamar said.

His eyes narrowed in an unspoken question. She sighed and stood up from her desk chair, her legs a little more unsteady than they should be. Amiran's eyes followed her as she walked past her mirror, past the doors of her balcony, to the narrow door in the corner.

'He used *that* door?'

'Yes.'

'But I thought you always kept it locked?'

'I do.' Except to let in the occasional lover – but it seemed better to stay quiet on that detail. He still believed she was a mourning widow, and he knew her well enough to have second thoughts about Anzor's death if the farce of her grief could no longer vouch for her innocence. 'He had the key.'

'He had *what*?'

'The key,' Tamar repeated. At once the full force of her exhaustion caught up with her, breaking free from those two treacherous words. 'Somehow he got his hands on the key to my room.'

Amiran blinked, his confusion tempering his anger and annoyance for the first time. 'You mean he made a copy of...'

'No. I mean that my own key disappeared from my room and showed up in the hands of a Taavi assassin.'

He stared at her. Tamar wanted to collapse, to sink onto the floor and curl to a little ball of fatigue, pretend none of last night's events ever happened and leave it to the rest of the world to sort out the mystery of her key's wanderings. But her knees wouldn't buckle, her spine wouldn't bend, and Amiran didn't even seem to think of asking whether she was anything near alright.

'You mean...' he began, visibly chewing on his words.

'Someone in the Red Castle wants me dead,' Tamar said.

She had come to the conclusion a dozen times last night. Now, spoken out loud for the first time, to the only man she dared to trust as much as herself, it sounded ridiculously unreal – *in* the Red Castle? One of her people? One of the servants or knights or lords or ladies she'd give her life to protect?

But Amiran didn't laugh that dry laugh of his. He didn't say it couldn't possibly be true.

'Oh, gods.'

'It's not just the key.' She gestured in the direction of the gate downstairs. 'He shouldn't even have gotten into the castle. One of the guards apparently let him in because he showed a letter signed with my seal.'

'Someone had access to your *ring*?'

'Apparently.'

Amiran stayed silent for a full minute, frowning at the hardwood floor; then he turned away and cursed.

'Yes,' Tamar said wryly. 'That's about my opinion, too.'

'It's madness.' He rubbed his hands over his face, leaving behind a stain of graphite just above the stubble of his auburn beard. 'Why would anyone at the Red Castle want you dead? Desperately enough to take the risk of breaking into your room, stealing that key, using your ring?'

'They may have bribed a servant to get into my room.'

'Doesn't really take away much from the point, does it?'

She grimaced. 'Admittedly.'

'Madness,' he repeated, shaking his head. 'You didn't do anything out of the ordinary, did you? And I don't assume Rusuvan's friends are so anxious to get him out of that trial that they'd rather send a Taavi murderer after you.'

'Don't you?'

He hesitated for a fraction, then glanced at her door and cleared his throat. Perhaps it was the wintry morning light, or perhaps he had really grown a shade paler. 'Hell's sake. How badly do you think Terenti wants to save his old comrade from the gallows, exactly?'

'I have no idea.' Tamar rubbed her eyes, but it didn't scrub her brother-in-law's face from her mind – a profile like a fighting dog, but an exceptionally bright one. 'He asked me yesterday to give Rusuvan a Lord's Trial, did I tell you?'

'What did you say?'

'That he could stick that Lord's Trial up his bollocks, in slightly politer wording. Which could have convinced him to switch to more desperate measures, in theory – but then again, he seemed quite confident I'd change my mind the next time we spoke.'

Amiran grimaced. 'If he had a murder planned, of course he'd take care to come across like he expected to see you again.'

'Admittedly.' She groaned. 'But it would mean he saw Rusuvan's arrest coming a month in advance and arranged for a Taavi assassin to be around in case I would be stubborn. He may have caught the rumours through his soldiers, but that still seems a *very* radical plan for just the possibility that—'

'Yes,' Amiran said. 'Don't see how anyone could have seen that coming, you being stubborn.'

'Piss off,' she said, unable to suppress a grin.

He shook his head, his laugh dwindling already. 'But I must admit – even if he wants to save Rusuvan, killing you would be unusually drastic. He's generally not...'

'No.' She couldn't claim she was on friendly terms with Terenti, but they had been allies often enough in the past decade – her as the wife trying to keep Anzor in check, him as the second son trying to minimise his brother's damage to the Sungarden family estates. They shared goals, usually. Rusuvan was an exception – but was even one of his oldest friends a reason to *kill* her?

For a man so pragmatic, so proud – perhaps. But she'd prefer not to believe it.

'Anyone else you angered in the past months?' Amiran said, following her line of thoughts.

She froze, momentarily unsure what to say. She could think of a couple of men she had angered – but was that possible, that one of her one-time lovers took to her rejection a little more dangerously than expected and resolved to take his revenge? Pridon, the duke of Sapphire Hill? Or that fellow from the Peaks – what was his name again? A shiver ran over her back. Hard to imagine that any of those impassive, indifferent creatures would suddenly turn hot-blooded enough to commit a murder. Then again, perhaps they just valued their pride more than her pleasure.

She'd have to figure it out somehow. Not through Amiran, though – and not through any other public channel, either, because she had no desire to let any of those men find out they hadn't been her only bedpartners in the past months.

'I can't think of anyone in particular,' she said. 'I suppose people are unhappy about specific decisions I have taken, but...'

'They *always* are. Nobody has killed you over it in fourteen years.'

Tamar shook her head and closed her eyes again. For the thousandth time her thoughts ran along every single complaint she could remember from the past six months – some dukes grumbling about taxes, a countess disagreeing with her daughter's elopement, the weavers' guild protesting the influx of cheap Androughan cloth. All of the usual noise, and none of it worth her head on a silver plate.

'Reziko may be able to figure out a thing or two,' she said. Although she should have a serious word with her Spymaster about this attempt on her life, too. She didn't pay him to let these things happen unnoticed. 'And speaking of spies – I might write to Rock Hall later today. If we're lucky, Jaghar and Viviette have the matter figured out by dinnertime.'

Amiran groaned. 'And if they haven't?'

She rubbed her forehead in a useless attempt to press back her headache. 'We still have the man himself, of course.'

'I suppose that's why you kept him alive?'

Tamar nodded.

'But how do you want to make him talk? He knows as well as we do that he's not getting out of the castle alive – unless you're planning to set him free in exchange for his information, but...'

'Wasn't really considering it, no.'

Amiran frowned, sinking his fists into her messy blankets. 'So how—'

'I'll think about it,' she interrupted him – too curt again. She couldn't help it. The thought of seeing eye to eye with the bastard again, of hearing that strangely persuasive voice again, was daunting enough to make her lose control of her tongue for a moment. He had *seen* her in those impossible moments of weakness, seen her on the brink of succumbing to that burning lust he evoked in her. He had *mocked* her. And then she was supposed to look him in those golden eyes again, to pretend she was still some unbreakable queen deciding over his life and death?

'You're not going to meet with him immediately, then?'

'Might as well let him sweat a little.' At least that would give her some time to pull herself together. 'I'll ask Reziko what he can find about him first – the more we—'

Knuckles on the door interrupted her. Amiran stood before she could tell him not to bother; he swung the door open with a brusqueness as if their visitor may well be the Taavi assassin himself. Instead one of her guards stepped in, looking unusually nervous even for a guard interrupting her private conversations.

'What is it?'

'Your Majesty, Your Highness.' The man bowed at her, then at Amiran, and swallowed. 'I – er – I was asked to pass on that your prisoner wants to speak with you.'

Tamar stared at him. Under her look, the man's face turned another shade paler.

'My *prisoner*,' she repeated slowly, 'wants to speak with me?'

'Yes, Your Majesty.'

'And did anyone already inform my prisoner that he, as a prisoner, is not in the position to want *anything*, let alone...'

'Your – Your Majesty – someone tried to kill him.'

She froze. 'What?'

'Someone tried to kill him last night.' The guard was stumbling over his words as if she would hang him in five heartbeats if he hadn't sufficiently explained himself by that time. 'When we went to check on him a moment ago – Gocha and Zviad and I – there were three arrows sticking into his bed. He says he hid underneath while someone shot at—'

Tamar closed her eyes, and he stopped talking.

'Go on,' she said without looking up.

'He didn't see his attacker, Your Majesty, because it was dark, he says – but he said he wanted to speak with you – well, he said you'd want to speak with him if you heard this – so we thought you might want to know—'

'Yes,' she said. 'Thank you.'

'Your Majesty, should we...'

Tamar opened her eyes. 'Guard the entrance to the dungeons. Keep him alive. I'll be with you in a moment.'

The guard bowed and scurried off. Beside the door, Amiran stood staring at her, perplexed lines around the corners of his mouth.

'For the bloody gods' sake.'

She didn't answer. The world was swimming before her eyes all over again – someone in the Red Castle. Someone *still* in the castle. Someone who had sneaked into her cells in the depth of night and fired three arrows into her prisoner's bed to prevent him from talking – and now the bastard wanted to speak with her?

'Tamar?'

'Yes,' she managed. 'Yes, we need to go see him.'

'If you'd rather not meet with him again...'

'Don't be nonsensical,' she said sharply. 'Of course I'll go.'

His sceptical look didn't escape her. Hell's sake, she should get herself under control – she couldn't allow him to find out how much of a mark the assassin left on her mind.

'Come,' she said, kicking herself into motion. 'No sense in waiting. Let's hear what he has to say.'

CHAPTER 5

'I must say,' Runo said, leaning back against the wall with his legs crossed on the floor, 'this is not exactly what I had in mind with the proverbial Redwood hospitality. Shooting arrows into unsuspecting sleepers sounds more like what we do in the Empire. Suppose I should be happy that you people are finally taking over some customs from the civilised south, but I wouldn't have started with *this* one, if I were you.'

The two guards standing beside his cell threw him a simultaneous murderous glare, and didn't respond. Runo sniggered and took another bite from the white bun they had handed him a few minutes before.

'Breakfast is pretty fine, though,' he continued, chewing. 'I'm only missing some fruit. If you could get me an apple tomorrow, that would be much appreciated. Or dried strawberries? Have heard it said that you have good strawberries in this part of the world.'

The square-shouldered guard by the name of Zviad looked like he'd quite like to shoot another few arrows into the cell. 'Do you ever shut up, Taavi?'

'Just trying to alleviate the boredom,' Runo said, which was true, if you considered nerve-wrecking tension a form of boredom. 'But I'll wait for Her Majesty in deep and utterly respectful silence, if that has your preference.'

Zviad just snorted, and didn't reply. His younger colleague – the round-faced boy named Gocha, who had been so eager to stick a sword through Runo upon his arrest last night – continued to glance at the corridor leading up every other heartbeat, waiting for his queen to show up and take over.

Not the most cheerful company. At least they brought torchlight and kept the murderers and the worst of his memories at bay – but their glares were a frightening reminder of how much reason Tamar had to kill him.

She's a murderer.

He let out an involuntary grunt. The two guards grabbed for their swords so quickly it was nearly comical.

'Thought you would be silent?' Zviad snapped.

'Does she do that a lot?' Runo said, ignoring that point. 'Killing people?'

'Why would you care?'

'Professional interest.'

Zviad snorted. 'She's not murdering people all over the place like that Empress of yours, if that was your question.'

Runo grinned. 'Are you certain of that, brother? Surely she didn't become the Iron Queen by smiling nicely at people.'

At least she killed *one* person too many. If he could find out who the unfortunate victim was, that might lead him to the identity of the masked avenger too – and he needed every little bit of information he could find if he somehow had to talk Tamar out of executing him.

'Look,' Zviad said brusquely. 'People died in the first year of her reign, yes? Her father – bless his soul – her father placed a lot of trust in the dukes and counts to reign their own territories. Then one of them killed him. Of course she had to reinstate some order.'

'By killing people?'

'She warned them once, and they thought they could ignore her. Hadn't realised she closed a marriage pact with the duke of Sungarden in the meantime.'

Runo raised his eyebrows. 'Anzor, I presume?'

'That's King Anzor for you,' Gocha snapped.

'Whatever you like – so she married him and had him murder her rebellious nobles for her?'

The young guard pressed his lips. 'The king brought the loyalty of a large part of the Redwood army with him.'

'Clever.' Exactly like the Empress did, marrying some chieftain from Gennekha to win over half the country at once. By the time the poor bastard died, two years and a son later, there had been no breaking free from the Empire anymore. 'How long had they been married when he died?'

Again Gocha had to force himself to even speak to him. 'Twelve years.'

Hm. *She's a murderer*. Little chance his helper-turned-assailant had waited twelve years to avenge some duke who got his neck stuck in a noose at the beginning of Tamar's reign. Runo scratched the back of his head and said, 'And in more recent years? Still so much murdering going on?'

'No,' Zviad groused. 'Are you shutting up now?'

Runo shrugged, shut up, and considered the options. Perhaps it *had* taken the masked traitor twelve years to realise that he could get outside help to avenge whoever Tamar sent to the gallows. More likely, these guards were simply unaware of a corpse or two.

He closed his eyes. The image of Tamar, naked and all too unwillingly willing, filled his mind's eye again.

She'd hesitated when she pressed that knife against his throat last night. Not enough of a hesitation to ignore the threat, but enough to know she wasn't used to the feel of a weapon in her hands. Which made it unlikely that she committed any murders by herself, in secret. The only clue that violence might have occurred closer to her –

The faint white spots on her arms. He would have taken them for innocent skin discolouring if they hadn't looked so painfully similar to the marks he had seen on former suspects released from the Empress's dungeons – burn scars. Someone had hurt her. Quite badly, too, on parts of her body she wouldn't show to the court in public. But if she had been burnt in private, she may have taken her revenge in private too.

He sighed. His creativity was running off with him. For all he knew she'd fallen into the last glowing embers of a fireplace as a child – perhaps fire was her father's idea of discipline, perhaps they were skin blotches after all. And even *if* she secretly killed anyone for burning her, then what? She'd be mad to give him that information. He wouldn't figure out who was after him this way.

What else did he have?

A secret. Her secret, more specifically. The loneliness catching up with her, rendering her momentarily desperate in his arms.

For a moment he couldn't suppress a faint smile, despite his clammy hands and the hollow feeling of approaching doom aching in his guts. No, he didn't think she'd been acting. Not entirely, at least. The question was how he would use that fact...

'Wipe that smile off your face,' Zviad snapped. 'The queen won't be here for your pleasure.'

'Sorry, brother,' Runo said, giving him a much broader grin just for the hell of it. 'It's hard not to smile at the sight of your pretty face.'

'Now will you—'

A door slammed shut in the distance, and Zviad immediately stiffened up. 'Stand for the queen, Taavi.'

'Make me,' Runo said, raising his eyebrows.

Neither of them seemed in the mood to enter his cell and force him to his feet. He was still leaning against his wall when Tamar sailed into the light of the torches, another man close behind her – probably a family member, judging by his dark auburn hair and the rather bloodthirsty stare he threw at Runo. A cousin? He vaguely remembered people had mentioned some cousin once or twice.

He sent back the brightest smile he could muster in the stinking cold of a Redwood death cell, and said, 'Good morning, Your Highnesses.'

'Your Majesty for you,' Tamar stoically corrected him as she stopped before his door and ran her gaze over the scene – the neatly folded blanket on his bed, the three arrows sticking from the wood. 'Well. Looks like you didn't have the most comfortable night, indeed.'

She sounded vaguely amused. Not like a woman who was planning on merciful gestures anytime soon.

'I've had them better, Your Majesty,' Runo said, meeting her gaze. A cold brown look – in no way resembling the hazed, lustful eyes that had blinked up at him from her blankets hardly ten hours ago. He smiled, pressing away the memories of his own arousal, and added with deliberate slowness, 'Then again, I've had them worse too.'

For a fraction of a heartbeat she froze, barely more than a flicker in her expression. Just enough to know he had hit the mark – *some* mark.

'Don't worry.' Her cold voice betrayed no trace of her hesitation. 'I'm quite sure I can make the next one more unpleasant, if that appears to be necessary.'

'Oh, I have all faith you can.'

She raised an eyebrow. 'Trying to flatter me?'

'Hadn't thought of that yet,' Runo said, tilting his head without releasing her gaze. 'But I could start, if you'd like – you look surprisingly radiant on this early morning, Your Majesty. A little more alive than I'd prefer, but absolutely... alluring.'

He saw Zviad's mouth sag open in the edge of his sight; behind Tamar, the cousin narrowed his eyes like a cat about to attack. Tamar herself didn't flinch, didn't even avert her gaze. Something dangerously vigilant blinked in her eyes as she held his stare for another heartbeat.

'Does that mean you'll be a little more accommodating today, Taavi?'

His grin broke through, unhindered by the burning glares of her company. So this was the game they were going to play? She wasn't going to pretend their conversation of last night had never taken place, wasn't going to deny the hands he laid on her?

'I might be, Your Majesty. What can I do for you this time?'

'Hell's sake,' the cousin muttered. 'Is he mad?'

'I'm not, thank you,' Runo said cheerfully. 'Not deaf, either.'

'I wasn't talking to you, you—'

'Amiran,' Tamar interrupted, her eyes still focussed on Runo's face, and the other man abruptly swallowed his words. His clenched jaw suggested it took an effort, though. Interesting, very interesting... Was she even commanding her family around? Really, he should have expected that too – he knew how the Empress treated her only son, at the rare occasions the boy even came home from his military campaigns.

'So,' he said, stretching his legs and ignoring the fuming Amiran entirely. 'What did you want to know, Your Majesty?'

'A report of the past night, to start.'

'Ah.' He gestured at the perforated bed beside him. 'I can't elaborate much on what you already heard, really. I was trying to fall asleep on this comfortable piece of furniture, heard a door, then a bowstring. Seemed reasonable to take cover by that time.'

'Do you know who attacked you?'

Zviad leaned forward in the short silence that followed, and beside him Gocha visibly held his breath. Amiran was still suppressing an obvious fit of anger.

'No idea,' Runo said.

'No idea at all?'

'None at all, Your Majesty. If there had been enough light to see him, he would have known I wasn't lying on this bed, you see.'

She clenched her lips. 'Did you hear anything?'

'Afraid not. Not every murderer in the world kindly stops by to introduce himself first.' He gave her a broad smile. 'I think I mentioned this before, but you really could have gotten worse.'

This time her pause was a full, audible one, long enough for her cousin to throw her a confused glance from behind her back. Still she did not look away, but for a moment her cold stare seemed softer, quieter, perhaps even a little hesitant.

It was in that infinitesimal moment that Runo knew his instincts hadn't betrayed him.

Because she shouldn't have hesitated, had she been acting last night. She should have laughed her empty laugh and told him to go fuck himself, perhaps in slightly more royal wording, and then continued her interrogation. She should at the very least not have looked, even if it was only for half a heartbeat, like she *agreed* with him.

He smiled. He couldn't help it. A warped triumph was rising in him, a sensation like that last, expectant turn before winning a game. A dangerous feeling to allow, sitting in a cell and staring down a queen not particularly known for her mildness. But she was still a little too beautiful, even standing straight like a soldier in her dark dress, her heart-shaped face frozen in that single indecisive moment. He remembered a little too well how her pink lips had parted last night, how she had softened under his hands. And even though she scraped herself together quickly enough, even though her gaze didn't soften, that moment of stunned silence suggested he might even come out of this confrontation alive if he played his cards right.

'Please leave it to me to determine how much or little I appreciate you, Taavi,' she said coldly.

His smile broadened all by itself. 'I confidently await your appraisal, Your Majesty.'

Now she looked away, abruptly as if she had burned herself, fixing her eyes at the arrows still sticking into his bed. 'Back to the point of our conversation. Even if you didn't hear or see him, you must know more about your attacker.'

'Wish I did.'

Tamar closed her eyes for a moment, like a teacher trying not to lose her patience with an extraordinarily stupid student. An excellent kind of exasperation. It proved she was losing that carefully created atmosphere of control – and better yet, that she knew it.

'I assume you agree with me that you were attacked by, let us say, the person who assisted you in getting into this castle?'

'That seems rather likely, yes.'

'In which case you should know who we're dealing with.'

Runo paused for a moment. He could just tell her the truth – I have not the faintest idea who we're dealing with, apart perhaps from a few useless observations that won't convince you to save my life. But that was a damn dangerous truth to just put out there. If he knew nothing, he was of no value to her; she might as well kill him immediately. The young guard beside her, at least, looked like he'd gladly take that task upon his shoulders.

She needed another reason to keep him alive. And the only card he had left to play...

That hesitation in her eyes. That apparent lie that may very well have hidden the truth in plain sight – *it's been pretty lonely since.*

He could think of more unpleasant strategies, he had to admit.

'And you think,' he said, leaning forward a few inches, 'that this is the place to discuss that question, Your Majesty?'

She raised an eyebrow. 'I quite do, yes.'

'In that case it seems we disagree.' He shrugged, without taking his eyes off her face. 'You may not have thought about it yet, but this attacker of mine clearly knows this castle and the people in it. Knows the cells well enough to blindly find the beds, too. Might be someone you're speaking with on a daily basis, someone your guards trust as much as they trust you. A single slip of the tongue is enough to tell this person exactly what you and I know or suspect about him, and I doubt you want to give him that much of an advantage.'

Her eyes sparkled with something that could be annoyance as easily as nervousness. 'What do you suggest?'

'I don't mind discussing the case with you,' Runo said. Quite the opposite. He didn't stand a chance if he couldn't get her to face him alone. 'But it'll have to be only you. I don't want anyone else around.'

Another fraction of silence fell before she bit out her mirthless laugh. Brought off balance again, even for the shortest moment.

'Do you honestly think I would even *consider* putting myself in the same room with you again?'

Runo shrugged and fell back against the wall. 'Good luck trying to find your traitor, then.'

She stared at him, her pink lips a thin line, the look in her eyes a strange mix between stone-hard fury and helplessness. Around her the guards and cousin remained silent. Yes, he could imagine that quickly became a lonely existence, surrounded by people who would only speak or act with her express permission.

'I'm trying to save my own skin here,' he added. He, at least, wasn't going to wait for her blessing to open his mouth. 'I know I wouldn't help myself by harming you. You don't have anything to fear from me.'

Not yet, at least. Not until he was out of here.

Tamar still didn't look away from him, her eyes piercing through him – trying to read his intentions from the back of his skull. Runo held her gaze, for what felt like minutes, until she nodded and stepped back.

'The doors will be guarded,' she said.

'Your Majesty!' the young guard hissed, his eyes wide with horror. 'You can't just leave him alone with you! He's tried to *kill* you!'

'If you kill me,' Tamar calmly continued, ignoring the boy, 'you will be arrested and put to death in the most painful way my people can come up with. Gocha, I trust you'll be able to think of a method or two.'

The young man swallowed. 'But Your Majesty...'

'Am I clear, Taavi?'

He shouldn't feel this triumphant. She was right, he would be stark mad to kill her in these circumstances. But at least he was one step closer to staying alive, one step closer to an escape from this death cell...

One step closer to a successful mission, after all.

'Crystal-clear as always, Your Majesty.'

She turned away from him without another word and gestured her men to follow. By the time she started speaking again, she was too far away for Runo to understand a word of it.

CHAPTER 6

They brought him into her working room chained and unshaven, his linen shirt torn at the chest and sleeves. Still the assassin stubbornly refused to look like a captive. Underneath the mess of his dark curls his eyes still mocked her, and his grin was still the grin of a cocky boy playing a game he can't imagine he'll lose.

Watch out, Taavi, Tamar thought. I've seen that grin before, and the man wearing it ended purple and choking on an unwelcoming granite floor.

Gocha kicked the prisoner in the back of his knees, forcing him to kneel before her. Even dropping onto the hard floor, the man wouldn't stop grinning that suggestive, leering grin at her. He didn't bow his head either.

'Your Majesty—' Gocha started.

'Thank you, Gocha,' she interrupted without taking her eyes off the scruffy, taunting face before her. A face that made her hands itch with the desire to slap the arrogance out of him – and yet she couldn't help but remember the steel command of his hands, the confidence with which he'd held her last night... Something stirred in her, and she feared it wasn't hate alone. 'You can release his hands.'

The guard blinked. 'But—'

'Release his hands, Gocha.'

He stood frozen for a moment too long, as did her men at the door. An unusual thing, for her commands to be ignored. She wondered, with detached amusement, if she was going madder than she even knew, if she was forcing these poor men to pick between her fury and that of her surviving next of kin. Then again, what did it matter?

'I'm not going to ask you a third time.'

Gocha knew the threat. Pressing his lips, he bent over, fumbling with the key to the heavy iron handcuffs. 'Your Majesty, if he hurts you...'

'He won't,' she said. 'He knows I'd take him with me to hell.'

The assassin's face split open in a derisive grin, but he still didn't speak a word, and didn't move his arms when his cuffs came off. Gocha stood up again, the chains in his hands, his mouth a tight line.

'But—'

'Enough,' Tamar said coldly. 'Get out. Now.'

He visibly suppressed a curse, but turned on his heels and marched out, followed by the two other men. Only when the door slammed shut did the assassin move, pulling his hands from his back and rubbing his wrists to get the blood flowing again. The sharp edges of the iron had left deep lines in his skin.

'They listen well to you,' he said. It sounded amused rather than complimentary. 'Do you publicly hang them if they protest?'

Tamar pinched her lips. 'If I need to.'

He laughed. 'Doesn't bode well for me. Or will you give me a chance to beg for mercy?'

She studied him for a moment. Even in the dirt of a prison cell, kneeling on her floor, he didn't give the impression he would ever lower himself to beg for anything. Then again, he also looked like a man who would do anything to survive.

'Would you grab a chance?'

'Of course I would. There's a reason I didn't make it to knighthood. Not enough honour in my body to die for someone else's principles.' He finally stopped rubbing his wrists and pulled his torn shirt straight. 'Do I need to stay here on my knees, Your Majesty? The floor isn't that comfortable, I must say.'

'Getting a knife into your chest isn't that comfortable either.'

'No. Then again...' He got to his feet with exaggerated groaning. 'You didn't allow me to slit your throat either.

So I don't see why I would allow you to force my knees to shit.' He grinned, then added carelessly, 'Your Majesty.'

Gods be damned, of course he wouldn't beg. He might speak the words, swear the oaths, deliver a picture-perfect show of a man pleading for his life – but he would do it all with that same twinkle of mockery in his eyes, and he would never grant her the obedience she had so painstakingly instilled into her court. Infuriating beyond belief – and yet she needed his cooperation, even if compliance was too much to ask. Someone had given him that key to her room. Someone in Redwood had been happy to see her dead, and if she didn't find out...

'What is your name?' she said.

'Runo.' He turned away from her, ambling through her room as if he were some high-born visitor admiring the books and accessories on her shelves. 'Nice library you have here. Don't think I've ever seen this many dictionaries in one place.'

'Who hired you?'

'Is that an original Bachana sword?' He reached out a murky hand. 'Could also kill you with this one, if you prefer. I would personally consider it quite an honour to breathe my last breath with an actual Bachana through my heart.'

'Keep your hands off my belongings. I asked you who...'

'Who hired me,' he finished, glancing over his shoulder. 'I heard you, Your Majesty. I'm just not answering you. You're not answering me either, after all.'

Tamar gave him a hard stare. He grinned a cheerful grin back and added, 'An answer for an answer. I'm not making any ridiculous demands, am I?'

Except that he was the prisoner here. Except that people didn't toy around with her, and *if* they did, she would make them pay for the offence, not give in to their demands, ridiculous or not.

But she *needed* his answers. She needed to know who had given him that key.

'It is a Bachana,' she said stiffly. 'Your time to answer, Taavi. Who hired you?'

'Taavi?' He laughed. 'Ah, yes. Imagine you'd stoop to using my name. To answer your question – I have no idea.'

'What do you mean, you have no idea.'

He shrugged. 'Key didn't come with a nice letter. And I wasn't going to ask questions if I could also just get my job done.' A glance of regret. 'Except that I didn't get it done, but that wasn't the key's fault, I suppose.'

'Then where did you get the—'

'Uh-uh. You're asking two questions in a row now, Your Majesty. That isn't according to our rules.' He stuck his hands in the pockets of his muddy trousers. 'So, my turn. Do you like it, controlling people?'

Controlling people? She hadn't felt so little in control for years; trying to hold authority over this man was like keeping water in a leaking bucket. Did he see it? Did he notice how clammy her hands had become, how weak her knees? He couldn't know. She couldn't betray herself – but good gods, if it hadn't hurt her pride so much, she'd have called her men for an old-fashioned torture session he at least wouldn't laugh at.

Although perhaps he would. She shouldn't assume anything with this man.

'I don't,' she said flatly. 'My turn, then. Where did you get the key?'

'A shady little inn downtown. Something with a stag's head, I believe? Wouldn't be able to say for sure. They all look the same.' He turned away from her again. 'If you don't like controlling people, why are you so hell-bent on doing it?'

'This doesn't have anything to do with our conversation,' she bit out. Her voice nearly trembled. Why was she so hell-bent on her people's obedience? Because she had seen how the court corroded from the inside out during her father's reign. Because she knew how the kingdom suffered when each duke made his own rules. Because she had known, seventeen years old and cowering under the weight of the crown, that they would grab every chance to put her out of action if she didn't pull the reins on them from the very first day. 'How did you know where you could get—'

'No, no, no.' He laughed out loud. 'Breaking the rules again. You didn't answer my question, Your Majesty.'

'I have no intention to answer your questions. Again, how did you know...'

'Fine,' he said, shaking his head. 'I will be merciful and ask you something else. But you'll have to answer one of them. I'm not going to spill my secrets if you're not willing to do the same.' He smiled at her, a dangerous twinkle in his eyes. 'Did you like it?'

Tamar nearly wavered. No need to ask what he was referring to; the skewed grin on his face told her enough. *Did you like it*? The damned impertinence – ambushing her in her own bedroom in the dead of night, leaving her no other defence than her own nakedness, and asking her if she had *liked* it – and yet, his forceful fingers, the strange tenderness of his touches...

'Of course I didn't,' she said sharply, interrupting her own mind before it could wander off. 'I had to survive. There was no other reason.'

'Oh, I know you didn't have another *reason*.' He waved her words away. 'Doesn't have to mean you didn't find it enjoyable.'

'I didn't.'

Runo turned around, fully facing her for the first time since he had started his round through her room. There was a nearly boyish cheeriness to his eyes, like some mischievous duke caught fondling another lord's wife rather than the man who had in all earnestness attempted to end her life a night ago.

'I think you did,' he said.

You've gone mad, Tamar wanted to say. How dare you. I hated your hands on me like hellfire. If you ever touch me again, I'll have you killed – slowly, and I'll be happy to watch every minute of it. But she knew as the objections welled up in her that she wouldn't be able to present a single one convincingly: she would be an actor reading her lines, no more convincing than the actor pretending to be in control that she'd been for the past ten minutes.

'You have some nerves, Taavi.'

'They come in the place of all that honour I lack,' he said cheerfully. 'I'm all nerves and a little madness. You don't seem to like it much.'

'Tell me,' she said through clenched teeth, 'how you knew where to get that key.'

He let the silence draw out a little too long. Then, nonchalantly, he said, 'I'm afraid I have a terrible memory. I really don't remember at this moment.'

Tamar let her breath escape in a long, terse hiss. 'In that case I'll happily ask my men if they can get some more information out of you. You're not doing yourself a favour by...'

'Oh, and neither are you,' he said, shrugging. 'My memory rarely improves under pain and fear. I suggest you try another method.'

'Any recommendations?'

'You could get out of that dress?'

She blinked, a good heartbeat too late. Even under his shameless grin she needed a few seconds to convince herself that her ears hadn't started malfunctioning – that he had suggested, loudly and clearly, that she undress herself in front of him. Like some street whore. Like some Taavi slave. Her mirthless laugh came out too baffled, and she couldn't help it.

'I hope you'll like the hot iron against your back.'

'Do you?' He turned around and sauntered to the other side of the study – coming, she realised a moment too late, between her and the door. Her skin started tingling in the small of her back. He couldn't hurt her, she had told Amiran three times in the past hour. Her guards would kill him if they found her hurt, and he wouldn't sacrifice himself in such a stupid way. But that rational, sensible argument only made sense for rational, sensible people, and by now she'd call the assassin lovable before she'd call him rational.

'You'll step away from that door,' she said, in her coldest, flattest tone. The tone her soldiers heard in their worst nightmares, Amiran joked. But the assassin only grinned, and stood where he stood.

Gods be damned. The illusion of authority was the source of all authority. The threat hovering over all suggestions of insubordination. The unspoken idea of all the harm she might do. Take that away, and what did she have? The small knife in her skirts? He wouldn't fall for that trick a second time.

Don't hesitate. Old reflexes kicked in. Don't show fear. Be self-assured, show that you *know* they won't hurt you, and perhaps they won't... She stepped forward, gaze a straight line despite her knees quivering under her skirts. Five steps to the door. He couldn't hurt her. If he hurt her, he'd hurt himself, and...

He stepped in front of her so quickly that she nearly jolted back.

From so close his broad body was a solid brick wall, reminding her far too sharply of his nearness last night.

He didn't pull his hands from his pockets. He didn't reach for her, made no effort to constrain her. But his muscles tensed up under his stained shirt, and he was no longer grinning.

'What are you going to do,' she snapped, 'kill me?'

'You have to admit, it's my job.'

'If you touch me with a finger…'

'Oh, I know, I know.' He sounded bored, but no longer so careless. 'Your guards will get me and I'll die a painful death, and so on, and so forth.'

'Then what do you want from—'

'I already told you. Get out of that dress.'

She had to look up to meet his gaze. Over the grim lines of his unshaven jaws, his eyes weren't laughing.

'And if I don't?'

He shrugged. 'Don't pretend you'd mind if I stripped it off you.'

Tamar uttered a sharp laugh. What game was he playing, for hell's sake? 'This is why you wanted to see me alone? So you could force yourself upon me and—'

'Force?' He sounded amused. 'You think very poorly of me, Your Majesty. Just because I kill people for a living doesn't mean I'll be looting women left and right too.'

'What – you think I'd *willingly* take off my clothes for you?'

For a moment he didn't move, answering her glare with an amicable, undisturbed smile. Then he said, 'Yes, actually.'

'You…' Words failed her for a moment – but was it because of the damned insolence, or because of the memories she read in his eyes? The knowledge of what he had seen? The feelings that had flooded through her last time she met his gaze from so close? 'You're digging yourself deeper and deeper into your own grave – you...'

'Not if you pull me out of that grave,' he said shrugging, and another baffled laugh escaped her.

'Why would I?'

'Because I'm about to make you a proposal, Your Majesty.' He still didn't look away from her – a gaze she could feel seeping into every quiet corner of her mind, unearthing a forgotten sensation of excitement, a danger so seductive it turned into temptation. A proposal. Nothing good could come from this man's proposals – but she had felt his hands on her body, that self-assured control, and for a moment that memory was far stronger than any sense of self-preservation. His voice was soft, a smooth, melodious siren's call. 'You don't kill me. In return, I'm staying silent on our naughty little secret. And if you ask me very nicely...' The corners of his lips perked up. 'I *might* even help you a little with that loneliness.'

'If I ask you *nicely*?'

His smile broke open to a full-blown grin. Tamar stepped back, away from him, her lips wavering between shocked gasps and a cutting laugh – still no way around his muscular body, no escape from this madness. 'This isn't *funny*, Taavi!'

'It isn't?' His grin only grew broader. 'I think it's pretty amusing, really.'

'You cannot speak to me like this.' Even the bitter laugh she forced from her lips couldn't come close to conveying the absolute ridiculousness, the impossibility, the flagrant disrespect in his words. 'You just can't. You...'

He took half a step towards her, his hands still in his pockets. 'Don't be silly, Your Majesty. If you hear me speak, obviously I'm perfectly capable of it.'

'And stay *away* from me.'

'Or else?'

Her breath stopped in her throat as he took another step closer – fear as much as the warmth stirring in her at the sight of his body, all hard muscle, all male pride. To her own disgust, wet heat blossomed between her legs, contrasting painfully sharply to the cold sweat tingling on her lower back. Or else? Else he may as well find out how much she wanted to accept his proposal, had it not been such an outrageous idea to allow an assassin – a *Taavi* assassin...

'Look at you,' he muttered, cocking his head aside. 'Take away the control, and what's left of you? Misery and loneliness?' A chuckle. 'The offer still stands.'

'You,' she bit out, losing control for a single damned moment, 'are the most arrogant – the most insufferable – the most—'

He shot forward, turned her against his chest and clamped a hand over her mouth, muffling the rest of her tirade. Tamar clawed for his damaged wrists, squeaking for breath, and found she might as well have tried to bend a steel beam; he barely even trembled as he pulled her tighter against him, branding her with the heat of his body. His free hand wrapped around her hips and drew her against a growing erection pinning her from behind.

Fight, her mind screamed at her. *Fight!* But her body, trembling between fear and desire, wouldn't move. Something else flooded over her – a need to give in, to succumb to the temptation of his strength. A need to give away, for once in her life, all control and command, to *let go*...

'The most what, Your Majesty?' he whispered, hot breath stroking her neck. His hand moved up over her stomach, rising slowly but steadily to her breasts.

Tamar swallowed, fighting the heat rising within her. He wasn't going to obey her. He was never going to obey her. And yet the thought didn't frighten her as much as arouse her – if he wouldn't obey her anyway, at least nobody could blame her for whatever was about to happen – for whatever she turned out to want.

A moan escaped her lips as he reached her left breast and cupped his hand around it with a tenderness she hadn't expected. He laughed softly behind her, taking his other hand from her mouth.

'I believe the word you're looking for is alluring, in case you needed suggestions.'

She opened her mouth to object, then gasped for breath as his fingers found her nipple under her dress and pinched it, sending a sting of both pain and pleasure through her. The assassin pressed his lips to the skin below her ear, both hands massaging her breasts now, and planted a slow trail of kisses along the lines of her neck – each of them hungrier than the last, as if he tasted the arousal on her skin. Again she couldn't suppress a moan. Her body was melting to his touch, thoughts turning inside out. Impossible. She *knew* this was impossible. She ought to scream, fight, set her nails into his eyes – but his fingers on her breasts kneaded the resistance out of her with such insistent tenderness, leaving only thoughts of more, of worse. The memory of his brazen hands clawing into the inside of her thigh. The hardness at his crotch, pressing against her lower back. She felt herself go slippery at the thought alone – oh gods, at least there would be nothing boring about *him*...

Something in her shoulders relaxed; her knees weakened. But the assassin caught her before she could collapse, spun her around in his arms like a willing rag doll and pinned her against him with only an arm around her waist. He gripped her bottom with his other hand, massaging the soft flesh with that same impossible, irresistible intensity.

'Now,' he whispered, 'ask me nicely.'

She jerked up her head to meet his eyes. A faint smile hovered around the corners of his lips. The world was turning around her, but his hands on her body did not give way – for hell's sake, an enemy. A murderer. She ought to struggle, even if she knew he would pin her down without effort. But no man ever held her this way, held her as if he could take the weight of the world from her shoulders, and her body refused to resist.

'You...' she began, fighting for words through the haze clouding her thoughts. 'I...'

He held her gaze, golden eyes shining with the amusement of a cat eyeing its wrestling prey.

'No.' Sparks of clarity, the last remainders of her sanity. 'No – I can't...'

'Oh, Tamar...' The hand on her bottom pulled her tighter against him, forcing her to feel every brewing inch of the bulge beneath his trousers. His smile was a devilish challenge, and yet there was no mockery in it – rather something that looked like... *encouragement*? 'You're making it so damn hard for yourself, aren't you?'

She opened her mouth. *I'm absolutely not*, her thoughts pressed her to say. *You're the one who's trying to kill me. I don't need your sympathy. I don't need your help.*

But no word came out.

'It's alright,' Runo whispered, lowering his face to her shoulder and brushing a gossamer kiss over her skin. She shivered, and couldn't stop shivering. 'You're lonely. I know you are. I know you don't want to admit it, but there's no sense in lying to yourself – you're lonely, you have been for too long, and you know exactly how much you need this...'

She squeezed her eyes, her breath catching in her throat. It didn't shield her from those delirious touches, his fingers circling around on the zone between her thighs and her buttocks, their strength obvious even through her skirts. It didn't make her forget about the promise of his erection pressing against her. It didn't keep out his voice.

'Let go, Tamar.' Captivating her, bewitching her. 'Stop swimming against the stream. Allow yourself to enjoy what you want to enjoy for once.'

'Please...' she breathed, and she no longer knew what she was begging for.

His breath stroked over her cheek as he rested his forehead against hers. She didn't dare to open her eyes. She knew what she would find if she did: full lips smiling their agonising temptation at her, golden eyes looking straight through every iron mask she had ever worn.

'Let go,' he repeated softly.

And his mouth found hers.

She kissed him back before her mind caught up, clung to his lips as if he were her last chance to live. He kissed her slowly, with nearly dreamlike intensity, his lips overpowering hers, dictating her every movement under their touch. The last resistance melted from her limbs. In some impossible way, he felt safe. He felt powerful. He felt –

In control?

She let go.

Her instincts took over, unthinkable instincts that overruled her rational mind with frightening ease. She lifted her hands and grabbed his lower back, finding only hard muscle and scorching heat below her fingertips. As she dug her nails into his shirt he groaned, clutched a hand around the back of her head, and drew her even deeper into their kiss. Her breath was his now, she no longer controlled even her own moaning voice. His wandering fingers set fire to everything they touched, the lines of her spine and the curves of her bottom and then finally the tingling skin of her thighs –

She gasped for breath. Runo groaned a laugh and moved forward, pushing her powerless body back until she bumped into her desk. Without breaking their kiss he lifted her onto the polished wooden surface and yanked her skirts out of his way, ignoring the pens and inkpots clattering to the floor behind her. Her bared legs spread around his hips as he moved forward, separating her thighs with his body. Still he didn't stop... With a purposeful move he pressed the bulge of his arousal against the soft flesh between her legs, grinding himself against her, sending flashes of agonising need through her loins. Tamar clawed into his shoulders, battling the urge to moan until she could no longer restrain herself. Again he laughed.

'Want me to stop, Your Majesty?'

'Don't – *toy* with—'

'Oh, trust me,' he muttered, running his fingers over her back until she shivered. 'I'm not toying at all.'

She felt nothing but his erection grinding against her, the heat that found her vulnerable skin even through his clothes. Her voice was unrecognisable, a hoarse, broken whisper. 'Then – oh damn you, what are you waiting for?'

'You.'

'What...'

His grin was all too obviously daring her. 'Ask me, Tamar. How often do I have to repeat it?'

She looked down, every fibre in her body focussed on his hard length rubbing against her, the unbearable tension throbbing through her. Oh, gods. Ask him. *Nicely*. Did he want to make her *beg* for him? But the warmth curling in her groin didn't care about shame and humiliation – her body knew only the raw power of his charm, the seduction of even his danger, the hollowness within her, begging to be filled. She wanted him. She wanted this. She wanted to lose herself for once, wanted to forget the world for once, and if she had to humiliate herself to get it...

He had seen the weakest of her anyway. There was nothing left to lose.

'Please,' she whispered, her voice a hollow rasp. 'Please – just...'

The assassin lifted a hand to her face, made her look up to him again. Honey-coloured eyes, looking straight through her, knowing every impossible desire hidden in the depths of her mind.

'Just what?'

'Fuck me,' she breathed. 'Please.'

Another smile tugged at his lips. 'Loosen my trousers.'

She should have laughed. She should have told him she wasn't taking anyone's orders, let alone his. But she had no pride left to salvage, and he made it so easy to obey...

Slowly, with uneasy hands, she let go of his back and reached for his buttons.

'Very well, Your Majesty.' He sounded nearly tender. 'Very well...'

Tamar unbuttoned his trousers, unable to look away from the bulging erection emerging under her trembling fingers. He was as large as the swelling of the linen suggested, as rigid and ruthless as the rest of him, looking like a deadly threat as much as a promise of pleasure. And yet her guts twisted eagerly at the sight of him, the knife in his hands forgotten.

'Look me in the eyes,' he said softly.

She followed the command as if she no longer had a mind of her own. At the same moment he laid his smooth tip against her slit, and she abruptly lowered her eyes again – oh, gods, to see all his hugeness aimed at her... But his fingers curled around her chin and made her meet his eyes before she could even gasp.

'Don't look away.' The intensity of his gaze burnt holes into her mind. 'I want to see you feel me.'

And he pushed forward and drove himself into her, his thick head stretching her open excruciatingly slowly. Never had she felt any man so intensely; as he advanced through her, inch after inch of her body ached to welcome him, then burst into flames as he filled all that had ever been empty within her. She wanted to close her eyes. She wanted to faint and feel nothing but his girth breaking through her. But he held her gaze, a stare like a predator, and she didn't dare look away from him.

'I – I feel you...' she breathed.

A smile. 'Barely yet.'

Her body seemed to wither in his wake as he pulled back, lowered his hands along her back and grabbed her buttocks to pin her in her place. She knew what was coming, she could feel it in his body tensing up – and yet nothing could have prepared her for his second thrust, splitting her open in a rush of heavenly delight. A cry fell over her lips as she arched towards him. Again he thrust into her, forcing her closer as he impaled her, and her body was no longer hers – his hands and cock owned her, and she could do nothing but deliver herself to the strange excitement of his uncontested control... He was everywhere. She was lost. The helplessness built to a terrifying tension inside her, pushed to higher and higher peaks with every thrust, until the pressure was so intense that she was sure her body would burst if he took her one more time. And still he didn't stop. Still he drove himself into her again and again to fuck the air itself from her lungs –

She broke without warning in an eruption of white light and breathless cries as the pleasure ripped through her and curled her toes and fingers. The assassin uttered a groan, hoarse and unrestrained, and slowed down, pulled back. In a reflex Tamar clawed her fingers into his lower back and yanked him closer, impaled herself upon him again as her body clenched around his girth. He sucked in a sharp breath. Dazed by the high of her release, she only heard that loss of self-restraint – saw his jaw tense and his lip curl up in a battle for composure. Again she pulled him closer. He groaned her name and grabbed her hips to pin her in place, his fingers tight with need. She let out a breathless laugh.

'Go on.'

'Tamar, I'm going to—'

'Go *on*!'

With a groan he thrust back into her, his forehead against hers, his fingers squeezing her hips, their lips close enough to kiss. She held his gaze as he rammed into her again, burying himself inside her sore, elated warmth. He still saw her, yes, but now she saw him too, saw him feeling *her* as he fucked her, saw him coming closer and closer to surrender. Saw something rising in his golden eyes that was nowhere near mocking – a sincerity, a desperation even, that lay so deep it hurt to look at it. With every thrust a grunt escaped his lips, hot breath stroking over her mouth and cheeks, his grip on her hips tightening...

He came with a tormented cry, his face contorted into a strained grimace, his hands clinging to her as he erupted inside her and flooded her with his hot seed. Then there were just his arms around her as she sagged against his chest, breathless and spent, her head a whirling void. Just the stability of him. Just his smell, warm spices and sunlight.

'Damn you,' he breathed, clutching her shoulders with shaking hands. 'You should know better, Tamar. You should know so, so much better...'

She was laughing before she could stop herself – wheezy, nearly hysterical shrieks of laughter rocking through her body. With a quick gesture he pushed her a few inches away from him, just enough to meet her gaze. An emotion she couldn't name flickered in his look, something stunned and inquisitive and vaguely dangerous. Something that wiped the laughter off her mind within an instant.

For a moment they stared at each other, eyes exploring the lines and shadows of each other's faces, and this time he was the first to avert his gaze.

'So,' she whispered. 'Not *everything* is a joke to you, then.'

He hesitated only for the shortest moment, then met her eyes again and smiled faintly. 'Might be. You'll never find out if you kill me today.'

"*Kill*... you.'

'As you were planning to.'

She stared at him, the first memories resurfacing from the whirlpool of her thoughts. Kill him, yes. She had planned something to that effect. Because he knew things. Because he could kill her too, if she wasn't careful.

None of which sounded even remotely true anymore.

'Tell me all you know,' she managed, and he lowered his face and pressed his lips to her sweaty forehead. She shivered.

He kissed her two, three times, then muttered, his lips still against her skin, 'And after I tell you?'

'After...'

She didn't finish her sentence. After he told her. After he was no longer of use to her. Kill him, she had thought – but how could she have him hanged now?

'I'll keep you alive,' she whispered. 'You have my word.'

He stiffened only for the shortest moment, then slowly ran his fingers over her shoulder and neck. In the delirious haze of those caresses, she nearly forgot to register his words. 'I don't know who's trying to kill you. Someone sent the Empress a letter, and the Empress sent me to go see him. He met me masked and hooded. All I know is that he comes from the Red Castle – but you probably figured that out by now.'

'That – that's all.'

'Afraid so.' His fingers danced around her jaw, then reached her chin. He trailed his thumb along the curve of her lower lip, his eyes focussed on the movement, his gaze charged with a concentration that sent shivers along her spine. Tamar closed her eyes. Fingers touching some part of her she had nearly forgotten, a part that wasn't a shield, that wasn't a disguise, that wasn't Queen Tamar of Redwood – a part that was just nakedly, vulnerably *her*.

'You really don't know – who betrayed me.'

'I'm absolutely useless to you on that point,' he said with a small chuckle. 'Then again, if I can be of service in any other way...'

He pressed his lips to hers before she could reply, and at the taste of him, the last of her self-restraint gave way again.

CHAPTER 7

E ven this underground dungeon suddenly no longer seemed so bad, the cold forgotten, the stench of death and rot merely a whiff of irrelevant memories.

You have my word.

Runo lay back on his plank bed and stared at the rock ceiling without truly seeing a thing. His thoughts were reeling, his body tingling. The triumph of a successfully executed plan, he told himself. But even while the thought emerged he already knew it to be a lie – if it had only been that simple, objective satisfaction, he ought to have felt the simple, objective dread of the barred door and the guard before his cell as well. But the fear could no longer get a hold of him through the warm glow that filled every inch of his body, the arousal that jolted through his cock with nearly painful stings whenever his thoughts turned back to the scene of that afternoon.

You have my word.

Tamar. Her fingers digging into his shoulders, her lips parted in breathless delirium. Her body clenching around him as she came. At the memory alone he was hardening already – hell's sake, he still wanted her. Wanted to pin her against her bed, or against her desk, or against some wall for all he cared, and fuck that desperate need for control out of her again...

'What are you grinning about?' Zviad snapped.

Abruptly the reality of the dusky cell pressed itself upon him again. Runo came up on his plank, forced the corners of his mouth down, and gave the guard his most harmless look. Something about the man's scowl suggested that "screwing your queen" wasn't the answer he wanted to hear.

'Just feeling grateful for all the pleasant company I've found in this place.'

'Oh, shut up.'

He chuckled, and shut up. Outside his cell, Zviad resumed his sauntering rounds through the corridor. Some three more hours to kill before another colleague would take over his shift. Keep an eye on him through the night, Tamar had ordered, and make sure nobody gets close to his cell.

Tamar.

You have my word.

Lying in his arms, spent and exhausted, she had been an entirely different woman than the queen who had, cold and fully dressed again, commanded her guards to lock him back up mere minutes later. But even as they took him away again, back to his cell, that look her eyes still followed him – bewildered brown eyes, seeing something...

Runo closed his eyes, a sliver of discomfort stirring. If he was honest, he wasn't entirely sure what she'd seen. *Not everything is a joke to you, then.* Which was true. Many things were futilities rather than jokes to him. Somehow he suspected that was not what she meant, though.

A disconcerting thought.

He barely suppressed a groan. Hell's sake, he was being nonsensical. *He* was not supposed to be the person losing his mind here. Fine, he had enjoyed this entire endeavour – had liked it a little more than he should have, feeling a force of nature surrender in his arms. And then what? Life was fun at times, just like it was hell at times, and none of it meant a damn. What did he think – that she would suddenly *like* him after all this madness? That it would win him anything to wonder what exactly she thought of him, except for the question of whether she would keep him alive another night or not?

Her word. With the haze of pleasant memories crumbling around him, that no longer sounded nearly as reassuring. Did he have any reason to trust her word? He knew how the Empress treated hers, and the damned fact that Tamar was ten times as beautiful didn't mean she would be any more merciful than any other tyrannical monarch around. She hadn't earned her moniker by gently patting her enemies on the head and requesting them to change their wicked ways. *She's a murderer.* She could change her mind about his life tomorrow morning – she could change it in an hour.

Good gods, he was an idiot. Why was he lying here and dreaming about her? He should be using the little time he had won to escape and finish his mission before she could get more unpleasant ideas about him. Somehow he had to get out. Find her. And...

Kill her.

As he had been instructed to do.

He knew his mission. Knew his own life depended on the success of it. So why did he feel that tangle of hesitation at the thought? It had never frightened him, killing. There was a strange kind of calm to it – not to the deed itself, which was always messy, and bloody, and noisy at times – but to the result of his labours, the stillness of death, the void of lifeless eyes. A blankness that felt like home more than anything else in the world.

Somehow he had an inkling it wouldn't feel like coming home to see the life seep from Tamar's eyes, though.

Runo rubbed his hands over his face, suppressing another groan. Stop it. He wasn't going to grow attached to the woman whose life he was supposed to end. He knew what was at stake – he would never see his home again if Tamar survived. Would never taste Orveli's almond cakes again, or see the blooming heather surrounding Raulinna, or smell the sharp, spiced fragrance of Taavi kitchens. He'd never hear the hauntingly beautiful songs of the Empress's attendants again. If Tamar didn't die...

And why would he *want* her to survive? It didn't matter an entirely different woman had emerged from behind that wall of cool composure – it didn't matter she'd looked at him with what was nearly *awe* for that single little moment, a look as if he wasn't some murdering bastard without a grain of honour in his body. She was still the same tyrant clinging to her power. She'd still figure out sooner or later that it made no sense at all to keep him alive. She was still the Iron Queen of Redwood – and according to his orders, the Iron Queen had to die.

One good screw wouldn't make him forget the life the Empress had granted him, would it?

He closed his eyes. Outside his cell, Zviad's footsteps were still making their slow rounds, coming closer and removing themselves again. Never too close to the barred door. No chance Runo could just grab him by the ankles in an inattentive moment and snatch the weapons from his hands.

And yet he *had* to get out. Sooner rather than later, if only because this sorry excuse of a bed would turn him into a crippled old man in mere nights even if nobody killed him before that time.

So how was he going to manage?

102

Around him the silence deepened as his thoughts finally found their focus again, that calm, quiet eye of the storm that always brought forth the best of his plans. Damn that masked bastard and his keys and letters. He should never have trusted anyone else's strategies in the first place. But it would be his mission from now on, his work, his decisions – the Empress would just have to accept it by the time he came home to claim that forty-third line in his skin.

Escape.

Kill Tamar.

Slowly the thoughts converged to a plan in the quiet of his mind.

A wiry guard showed up to take over Zviad's post some two hours later, by what had to be the early evening. The man brought a piece of hard bread and some dry cheese with him – still no strawberries, Runo concluded with some regret. But food was food, and he would need the fuel for the rest of the night.

He ate in silence, ignoring the guard as he chewed and tried to look like a man who wasn't planning anything unpleasant. Then he stood up and paced back and forth through his small cell, in what felt like a decent imitation of Zviad's never-ending rounds – frown on his face, eyes focussed on the floor, deep in thought for anyone who'd see him. Fifteen feet away, the guard didn't speak. Yet when Runo abruptly stopped at the iron bars of the door, the other man looked up with too much suspicion to pretend he hadn't been following every step and gesture.

'What?'

'I just thought of something,' Runo said.

He made sure to have it sound a little dazed, wondering how in the world he could have missed this particular memory so far. At the other side of the corridor, the guard cocked his narrow head and repeated, with obvious sarcasm, 'Something.'

'About your traitor. The fellow who's trying to kill your queen.'

The other stayed silent now. Runo muttered a curse and fell back on his plank bed, rubbing his hands over his face. When no questions followed, he added a few muttered words in Taavi that he assumed a simple Redwood guard wouldn't be able to understand – but at least they'd sound appropriately alarming. His efforts didn't remain unnoticed.

'Well, what is it, then?'

Too sharp. Too fast. At least the man was a *little* concerned. Runo looked up from his hands and said, 'I can hardly tell *you*, brother.'

'Why wouldn't you—'

'Told your queen I wouldn't discuss what I knew with anyone.' He forced a grin. 'Not particularly looking forward to her reaction if I break that promise.'

That argument convinced the guard faster than he'd dared to hope. Another clue that he really shouldn't rely on her merciful feelings.

'Well, fine, I'll go ask her when she wants to—'

'What do you mean, you'll go?' Runo interrupted him. 'Seem to remember she gave orders to make sure I wouldn't be left alone for even the shortest moment.'

'Come on now.' The other man scoffed. 'Nobody'll kill you in those five minutes.'

'That's what they thought about last night as well. Do you really want to risk it, coming back to find me dead in my cell just when I figured out a thing or two about – well, the whole situation? Don't think she'll be particularly happy about that either.'

The guard stared at him, apparently dumbfounded by this series of complications. Runo sighed and shrugged, carefully maintaining the impression he was thinking the matter through for the first time now.

'I suppose you could take me with you.'

'Take you *with* me?'

'Don't look that shocked, brother – I'm just—'

'Not your brother, you bastard.'

Runo sniggered. 'Whatever you prefer. Look, I'm really not planning to cause you any trouble. She's keeping me alive for now, I'm not going to give her a reason to change her mind. But she'll want to know what I know. And she'll want you to keep an eye on me. So as far as I can see, this is the only solution that won't have her put us both to the gallows.'

The silence was tangible. An interesting novelty, really, to threaten an opponent with someone *else*'s anger. He could see the dilemma play out in the other's expression. What was the man supposed to do? Wait until a colleague came down and risk Tamar's anger for not notifying her sooner? Leave his prisoner alone and risk Tamar's anger for endangering his life? It really left him with very few options.

He muttered a curse. Runo nearly laughed.

'Sorry for the trouble, brother.'

'I told you not to call me...'

'Fine, fine – are we going to see Her Majesty, then?'

A last hesitation, then the guard groaned and grabbed for the keys at his belt. 'Get back against the wall.'

With a shrug Runo stepped to the farthest wall of his cell, no more than ten feet away from the door. The guard didn't take his eyes off him as he wrestled with his keyring and fumbled the key into the lock with one hand, clutching the hilt of his sword with the other. Even from the distance, the lines of tension around the man's beady eyes were more than visible.

Runo had to make an effort to keep the corners of his mouth down. Even the most reassuring of smiles probably wouldn't have the desired effect here.

At long last the door opened, and the guard moved back, drawing his sword. 'Turn around with your hands on your back.'

Runo obediently turned, leaning his forehead against the cold, slippery stones. Behind him he heard the guard come closer, keys rattling at his belt, breath heavy with tension – enough noise to determine his location by the inch. Two more steps. One more. The clatter of iron handcuffs. This was the moment where any sensible fugitive would turn and fight, Runo knew –

So he didn't turn.

Instead he lunged backwards, moving blindly in the direction of the panting and rattling, his hands still behind his back. Almost immediately he found chainmail and leather under his fingers, a body too stunned to react for the shortest of moments – and it was in that moment of frozen reflexes that he *did* turn around, sent his fist flying at where he expected to find a face, felt the bones of a nose splinter under his knuckles. A dazed scream of pain. Handcuffs clattering against stones. In the edge of his sight Runo saw a sword-arm come up, hopelessly late – but he stood too close to stab now, and blocked the swing with a hand around the guard's iron-clad wrist. For two, three heartbeats their wrestling bodies were all his mind registered, stubborn muscle and desperate resistance, the smell of cold sweat blocking even the stench of rats and rotting bodies. Then he found the weakness, no more than a slight unevenness in his opponent's steps. A sharp kick in the shins did the rest of his work. The guard screamed again, wavered for a heartbeat too long. Runo clawed his fingers into the man's shoulders and slammed his heavy body head-first into the rough wall.

The last scream abruptly died away. The sword clattered against the floor, and the guard's unconscious body folded like a rag doll as he sank down beside his weapon.

Runo stepped back, fire buzzing through his veins. It took him a few moments to get his heartbeat back under control, to check if all his limbs were still intact, if he hadn't missed the pain of a cut in the rush of the fight – but apart from a few sore spots that would be bruises in an hour, he seemed unharmed. With compliments to good old Porvo, he thought wryly, who spent so many hours training him under Raulinna's merciless summer sun. A pity the Empress ordered the man to chug down a glass of belladonna two years ago, after hearing the rumours of his affair with one of her personal slaves.

Runo forced himself to shrug as he sat down on his plank bed. Old bastard should have known better than to get attached to the girl.

He pulled the guard's limp body closer and tugged the chainmail, heavy leather boots, and belt off his body. The shoes were a little too big on his own feet, but he'd just have to deal with it for a few hours – his lighter Taavi boots drew far more attention and would betray his identity even to the densest of servants up there. The chainmail, on the other hand, fit pleasantly well. With a suppressed groan he got back to his feet and buckled on the belt. Ready to go out, except for the last question –

What to do with the man at his feet?

For a moment Runo stared down at the unconscious face, with the calm, cold resignation he knew so well. The calm of a life about to end. At most missions he wouldn't have hesitated. If he killed the man, at least he didn't have to worry about an early alarm, guards drawn closer by his shouts.

But this time...

Convincing Tamar to keep him alive was easier if he never killed a single soul on Redwood soil. And of course he wasn't planning to rely on her goodwill again. He should just finish the mission and be out before midnight. But it could never hurt to keep the consequences of failure in mind, and if he was caught, if he had to face her again – he'd quite prefer for her not to feel more revengeful than she already might.

With a feeling that came close to regret, he turned away from the guard's body and snatched the sword from the stony ground. He locked the door behind him and stuck the keyring into his pocket. He rubbed a handful of dust over his face, just enough to obscure his features at first glance, his noticeable Southern skin, some of the stubble on his cheeks.

Then he made for the door through which he'd entered the cellars. Time to find Tamar – again.

CHAPTER 8

Howin the world was she supposed to ever work at this desk again?

It took Tamar two hours to finish her letters to Tanglewood Castle and Rock Hall, short as the notes were – two hours in which she could barely reach for her inkpot without remembering how it had fallen onto the floorboards as the assassin positioned her on her desk. At every creak and rustle her fleeting mind expected the study door to open; the odour of the Taavi's body still hung faintly in the air, a whiff of sweet musk whenever she inhaled too deeply. Even her fingers no longer seemed willing to obey her. She ruined three sheets of parchment with ink blots and slipped lines, and even the letters she eventually folded and sealed contained twice as many crossed mistakes as any of her usual writing.

Now Lasha was sitting on the other side of that same desk, droning on about requests and decisions in that low, nearly masculine voice that made it far too easy to drift off and think of golden eyes and tender fingers instead. 'The duchess of Old Arches objects to your tax raise from seven to nine percent on her personal income and asks for a reconsideration, Your Majesty.'

'Make it ten,' Tamar said, closing her eyes. She still felt the Taavi's hands on her hips, his lips devouring her; it took an effort to keep her voice level. 'And tell her it will be twelve if I hear about it one more time.'

'Thank you, Your Majesty. Then – let me see, Lady Niza asks for your intervention on behalf of her son and his—'

Tamar interrupted her with an annoyed gesture. 'As I've told Lady Niza twice already, she should double her ransom offer. I'm not going to waste any favours Andrough owes us on an idiot who should have known better than to fool around with warlords' wives.'

'Noted, Your Majesty – that was all I had on my list.' Lasha produced a cautious cough, her angular face a little more nervous. 'Do you wish to write anyone about the assassin?'

'About the...'

She lost track of her words again. The Taavi. The *damn* Taavi. Even while he sat locked up in a cell deep below the Red Castle, his voice still sang at her from the walls of her working room, repeating impossible truths in that mesmerising baritone. *You're lonely – making it so damn hard for yourself – stop swimming against the stream...*

A shiver ran through her. Her body betraying her once again.

'I'm still considering my thoughts on the assassin,' she said, and somehow her voice didn't waver. 'See to it that my letter to Jaghar and Viviette is sent out as soon as possible, will you?'

'Very well, Your Majesty.'

'Thank you, Lasha. That was all.'

Her secretary gathered her notes and letters and vanished, closing the door behind her as she stepped out. Tamar sagged in her chair as soon as the lock clicked shut and suppressed another shiver – the assassin. Good gods, she had to scrape her mind together. At the very least she had to stop thinking of him, of the startling gentleness of his touches, the sensation of his golden eyes watching her. *Seeing* her. As if he cared, as if...

'Oh, *stop* it!'

Her voice echoed back at her in the stillness of the room. She closed her eyes and buried her face in her hands. What in the world was she thinking? Of course he didn't care. He was a *Taavi*. An insufferable, arrogant bastard with no care in his life except the occasional murder. Had she really believed for a moment that he gave a damn about all those thoughts he read on her face so easily? He was just playing games, like they all did in the Empire – trying to bring her off balance, and succeeding far too easily. She gave him her *word*, for hell's sake. What had she been thinking?

Someone knocked at her door, the tapping of fists on wood too loud in the silence. Tamar jolted in her chair. Again she expected for a moment to see the assassin ambling in – but the door remained closed, waiting for her permission.

A leaden tiredness washed over her as she forced herself to her feet. If only people could give themselves their permission every now and then, at least she wouldn't have to deal with them all the time.

She opened the door nonetheless. If she didn't keep an eye on people, the gods knew what madness they would come up with.

'Your Majesty?' The girl on her doorstep curtsied so deep that Tamar thought she'd never get up again. 'Apologies for disturbing you, Your Majesty – a few people ask to see you.'

Of course a traitor in the Red Castle wasn't enough. Of course they wouldn't grant her a day off – worse, they probably hoped she'd be distracted enough to do their bidding for once.

'Send them through,' she said. 'And tell them to be succinct, whatever they have to say.'

The girl curtsied again and hurried off. Tamar left the door on a chink and sank back into her chair, staring at the grey winter sky outside. The first pair of footsteps approached in the corridor within minutes.

Not the Taavi assassin – she managed to suppress that faint hope by now – but to see Pridon of Sapphire Hill appear in her doorway was double the disappointment.

'Come in,' she said curtly. 'And close the door behind you.'

Too late she realised he might take that as a hint that she'd be open to the resumption of activities the rest of the world wasn't supposed to know about. With the scorching memory of this afternoon still tingling on her skin, the thoughtless dreariness of his lovemaking seemed more repulsive to her than ever before.

Waving a demonstrative gesture at the chair furthest away from her desk, she added, 'Take a seat.'

A sharpness slid over his smooth face again, like when she'd told him to leave her room in the middle of the night. Still he didn't object as he sat down.

'Well,' Tamar said, folding her fingers. 'You wanted to speak with me, my lord?'

'Oh, please just call me Pridon,' he said, and chuckled with a little too much joviality. 'I'd say we're quite past the my lord and the—'

She sighed. 'As you prefer, but I don't suppose you're here to discuss our mutual forms of address.'

'No, no, of course.' He paused for the slightest moment, an obviously deliberate hesitation. 'I – well, obviously I heard about the events of last night. Very distressing. You've been unfathomably lucky.'

You could have gotten way worse. Something stirred in her stomach again.

'I'm well aware.'

'Ah. Yes, of course you are.' He chuckled again. 'I was considering, you might be helped with some reinforcement of the military force at the Red Castle. The gods know how many of these dogs the Empress might send after you – not to frighten you, of course...'

Tamar closed her eyes for a heartbeat. His wording was so circumspect, his tone of voice so infuriatingly watchful – and yet that gleam of satisfaction in his eyes told her he didn't give a damn about her fear and distress, that none of this was about helping her. Under the weight of her exhaustion, it took all she had not to point out the exit and tell him not to show his weasel face to her for the coming year at least.

'I'm not frightened, Pridon, thank you.'

'Ah.' He sounded undeniably disappointed under his thin veneer of surprise. 'Nonetheless, you'll doubtlessly agree that it's better to have too much security than too little, under these circumstances? My men in Sapphire Hill are mere days away. I'll happily send a few of them to the Red Castle, if you'd appreciate the help.'

The last part of that sentence came out with obvious satisfaction, and again he looked far too pleased with himself – if she'd appreciate the help. If she was willing to grant a favour in return, the words between the lines said. If she would perhaps reconsider her refusal to see him again, because really, wouldn't it be rather thoughtless to shove a man out of your bedroom after he went to such lengths to protect you from foreign murderers?

'Considerate of you to think of it,' she said coolly, 'but it seems to me we have exactly the right amount of security around at the Red Castle. He didn't manage to kill me, after all.'

'You have to admit he came close, for—'

'Oh, certainly. I didn't say it was an abundance of security.' She gave him a cold smile. 'But it seems to have been enough, and I wouldn't want you to exhaust your resources for no good reason. Was that all?'

The duke stared at her, the expression on his slick face no longer so careful. 'I see. That was all, yes.'

'Thank you for your consideration, in that case, and please be so kind to send the next in line this way.'

He brusquely stood up and made for the door in five terse strides. Only with the doorhandle already in his hand did he stand still and turn back to her, his upper lip tense to the point of curling up.

'You might change your mind. The offer still stands.'

'Much appreciated,' Tamar said, well aware that neither of them would believe the lie. He bowed the most minimal bow in the history of mankind and disappeared, slamming the door a little too loud behind his back.

She closed her eyes again and cursed. The silence of her room stared back at her, blank and uncaring.

So what was she supposed to make of this offer, then?

Someone in the Red Castle sent the Taavi assassin after her. Someone who knew about that second door to her room, someone who had access to her ring or the money to bribe a servant for it. Pridon fulfilled both requirements – so could this be the plot? Send a murderer into her bedroom to either take revenge for the humiliation of a few months ago or to scare her into accepting his help, and eventually his advances?

Or was she seeing ghosts now?

But before she could calm her mind knuckles sounded against the door of her working room again, and this time her visitor came in without waiting for her answer.

'Do I disturb?'

'Oh, Terenti.' She sank back down in her chair, suppressing the urge to tell him he did, indeed, walk in at a rather inopportune moment. He still determined the loyalty of the Sungarden armies for which she suffered twelve years of Anzor, and if she was unlucky, he might well know more about the knife that nearly ended up in her chest last night. Better not to upset him any more than she had already done. 'Come in.'

Her brother-in-law nodded, closed the door behind him, and took a seat without waiting for her invitation. As always it took her a moment of effort not to shove away from him. Not that he resembled Anzor so closely – he was built stockier than her dead husband, wore his hair longer and his beard shorter. He dressed in the simple leather and chainmail of a soldier, too, rather than the richly embroidered velvet Anzor preferred. But in his eyes she recognised that same flicker of ruthless pride, that same fierceness that could easily grow into meanness, and it was exactly that flicker she had learned to watch out for in the first few months of her marriage.

The last thing she wanted to think about, with her mind still besieged by the Taavi's impossible passion.

'Hope you're doing well?' Terenti said, interrupting her thoughts. 'Must have been a shock.'

For a short, ridiculous moment she wondered how he would react if she told him about the full extent of the shock – he fucked me, Terenti. He fucked me right on this very desk, where you're resting your elbows at the moment, and I enjoyed it more than I ever enjoyed your brother in the full twelve years of that torment of a marriage...

At the very least it would shut him up about Rusuvan's court case for a moment.

'Quite a shock, yes,' she said flatly, restraining herself. 'But we're looking into the matter. We'll figure it out soon enough.'

'Glad to hear.' This, the tone of his voice suggested, was more than sufficient for the empathic part of the conversation. 'I suppose you don't mind me asking a few questions about the Tanglewood matter?'

Suppose you don't mind, his voice echoed in her mind. You're iron, after all, and iron never cracks. Let's chat about political intricacies, mere hours after you could have died – who needs a moment of rest after an assassination attempt, anyway?

'Not at all,' she said.

The alternative, after all, was admitting that she *did* crack. The illusion of authority – she knew how the vultures would react to the slightest hope of wriggle room.

'Wonderful.' Terenti crossed his legs and leaned back in the chair, suddenly all businesslike stoicism, all diplomatic efficiency. None of Pridon's cowardly slickness – he spoke his words with cold purpose, like a wall advancing on her. 'I suggested yesterday afternoon that it may be better to grant Rusuvan a Lord's Trial rather than the usual judges – did you have time to consider that option this morning?'

For hell's sake. She barely had the time to eat *breakfast* this morning. But she sighed and said, 'I think I was clear about my opinions yesterday, wasn't I?'

'I was hoping you'd think the matter through with a fresh perspective. You must realise I'm not the only one who's a little concerned at the way Rusuvan is treated. The man ruled that duchy for nearly two decades. A few irregularities are to be expected in that time – and to see how he's discarded despite—'

'Would I find hundreds of silverlings disappearing into nothingness if I checked your cash books, Terenti?'

He frowned. 'I hope not, but—'

'Have any of your concerned friends experienced these kinds of irregularities, then?'

'Not that I know, but that is beside the point, isn't it?'

'I'd say it is the point,' Tamar said, raising an eyebrow. 'If none of you have to deal with similar issues, we can conclude that Rusuvan should at least have been able to prevent them. Or would you suggest he's so inherently incapable that he cannot be blamed for whatever faults were found in his administration?'

'Not at all. But as I said – you seem to assume in advance that he must be guilty, and that's rubbing some of us the wrong way. Your only source seems to be a young woman fully under the influence of a husband who was exiled from Ulrick's court, for hell's sake. You have to admit it's an unpleasant idea that you may as well throw *me* into a dungeon tomorrow as soon as one barely capacitated family member accuses me of fraud.'

'That's not—'

'And he *may* be guilty,' he interrupted, speaking louder now. 'That's exactly what the jury is supposed to decide during that trial, isn't it? But you'd avoid a lot of unnecessary resistance by giving him a fair chance, at least.'

'A fair chance? By allowing his old friends to assess the evidence against him?'

Terenti scoffed. 'Do you really think that would influence me?'

'Not you, perhaps.' A lie – they both knew. 'But can you guarantee to me that all members of that jury would be so impartial?'

'We'll take care to select...'

We. The control was, slowly and subtly, being pulled from her hands. Don't worry, Your Majesty, we'll take care of it – here's the jury we hand-picked from a selection of his old friends, here are a few clever arguments about irregularities we all have to deal with, and we've set him free already to spare you the hassle of looking into the case. Her voice turned sharper by itself.

'You won't be selecting anything or anyone now.'

His bulldoggish expression hardened. 'I'm trying to spare you a handful of grudging nobles, Tamar. With all this assassin trouble going on, I assumed a horde of complaints about this case was the last you needed.'

How awfully fortunate again, that assassin roaming through her castle. Seeing ghosts – of course she was seeing ghosts – but *someone* must have betrayed her.

'Considerate of you to take my wellbeing into account,' she said, looking up to meet his eyes. Too much like Anzor's. Her heart cramped in her chest. 'I suggest we leave the matter at this for now. I'll write to some other parties involved to hear their opinion, then I'll let you know what I decide to do.'

'There's no—'

'You've made your point, Terenti.'

His lips clenched to a thin line, but he nodded and stood up without another word. 'Wishing you wisdom in your considerations, then.'

Perhaps she wouldn't have heard a threat in those words if an armed man hadn't broken into her room last night. Perhaps she would just have taken them as the thousandth insincere wish passed between them. But she couldn't ignore the biting suggestion behind that innocent sentence now – you'd better be wise, Tamar, because you'll suffer the consequences if you aren't.

'Thank you,' she said. 'We'll speak later.'

Three more of them followed until she could finally retreat to her bedroom, too exhausted to even think of dinner. At least on her bed she wasn't forced to think about the madness that had made her kiss a murderer in her own damned castle, that had made her unbutton his trousers for him –

Then again, her bedroom reminded her twice as sharply of his armed entrance of last night, the words she should never have heard. *You've been lonely for a very long time, haven't you?*

She closed her eyes and sank down in her blankets. Her body felt like a stiff cage, a cold, dead thing she was dragging along out of pure necessity. Lonely. Surrounded by people who either forgot she still had a heart beating in her chest or didn't give a damn about it, bloodsuckers and vultures, pressing and prying until she'd give in, or until she'd die resisting. Someone from the Red Castle. Someone who knew the castle well. The assassin had been right – it might very well be someone she *trusted* –

The door flew open.

Amiran stormed in, Gocha following in his wake with his sword in his hand. Outside her room Terenti's voice was shouting commands at other guards, his words obscured by the noise of running footsteps and clattering weapons.

'What?'

'Oh, thank the gods.' Amiran stumbled to a standstill in the middle of her room, panting. His normally

impeccable clothes were rumpled, his face flushed.
'Here you are. Tamar—'

'What in the *world*...'

'Tamar, he's out.'

She stared at him. Behind him, Gocha's eyes were
flying from her to the door and back to her, his thin nose
trembling, his fingers clutched so tightly around his
weapon that his knuckles turned white. Now she could
distinguish Terenti's words on the corridor – 'Don't
bother keeping him alive! If you find him...'

'Out?' she said hoarsely. 'How?'

'Knocked his guard out. Gocha just found him at the
change of watch.' A quick nod at the young man behind
him. 'What do you want us to do? I've posted men at all
your doors. Terenti is combing the castle, we should be
able to find him. Anything else we should think of?'

Tamar opened her mouth and didn't manage to bring
out a sound. Out. Escaped. After she had promised not
to kill him – after *he* had...

'Keep him alive.' The words fell from her lips without
thought. 'Tell Terenti not to kill him under any
circumstances.'

Amiran frowned. 'You said he didn't know anything
useful?'

'He must know more than he's telling me.' Her voice
came up with the lies by itself, and she didn't have the
brain left to stop it. All she knew, with unsettling clarity
under the harshness of Terenti's commands outside,
was that she didn't want him to die – that she wouldn't
be able to bear the sight of his corpse now, his strong

hands frozen in the rigour of death, his golden eyes empty. 'I want him alive at least until I've heard from Jaghar and Viviette.'

'But he—'

"*Amiran.*'

Her cousin stood frozen for a moment, then muttered a curse and strode out without another word, slamming the door behind him. It left only Gocha standing in her room, trembling and clutching his sword as if he were about to commit a murder.

For a moment her gaze nearly met the boy's. He lowered his eyes immediately, so brusquely it nearly looked violent.

'Your Majesty.' He seemed to be struggling with the words. 'Is there anything I can do?'

Her breath felt like ice in her throat. Say something kind, she wanted to beg. Don't stand there awaiting my instructions like you don't have a mind of your own – you can *see* it, can't you, that I'm as frightened as you are, confused and exhausted and still alone? Can't you at the very least ask me if I'm alright? Suggest you'll bring me a cup of tea, or give me a hug for all I care – just do *something* without my explicit orders?

He hadn't waited for her orders, at least...

'No, thank you,' she managed. 'Just keep me safe, will you?'

A shadow slid over his young face, but he nodded and vanished with a last bow, leaving her room empty and drenched in icy silence.

Tamar sank back into her blankets and clenched her hands until her nails cut through her skin. Around her the world was turning. Escaped. He had *escaped*. And what else did you expect him to do, the voice of reason told her. You know who he is, you know whose orders he follows. But that small spark of unreasonable hope had pushed her through the afternoon, the dream, no matter how naive, of someone who would *care* for once in her life – and now...

Faint shreds of the noise outside still found their way through even the thick wooden door. Keep her safe. They'd keep his knife away from her, yes, but how would they save this cold, dead heart of hers?

She curled up to a little ball in her bed, wrapped her arms around her knees, and buried her face between them. There, hidden from the watching eyes of the world, the tears finally came.

CHAPTER 9

Sitting in the cold darkness of the winter night, Runo waited until the cover of clouds finally dissolved around the waxing moon above his head. Only then, in the faint silver shine that at least allowed him to see his own hands, did he get up from the wall where he'd spent the past four hours in silence, huddled under a handful of blankets he pulled from some deserted room on his way up.

They would be searching for him now. The guard would have been found. But so far nobody had been bright enough to take a look at the balcony two floors above Tamar's room, or noticed the peculiar absence of a coil of rope from the stables, or missed the knife he'd snatched from the armoury in the falling twilight of this cloudy evening.

His mind was crystal clear, brisk and light like the cold winter air. He knew what he was doing again. He was doing what he did best again, what he should have been doing all along in spite of all masked traitors offering him easy plans and clever lies – the calm, purposeful execution of a strategy he knew well enough to follow it sleeping. Quickly but quietly he bound the rope to the iron railing of the balcony, three knots and a fourth to be sure. He stretched his body for a few minutes until the blood was streaming in his fingers again and every inch of him felt warm and awake and strong enough to hold his own weight. He checked the lock on the door behind him one last time. He checked the knots and the knife at his belt.

He wrapped the rope around his wrists, flung the loose end down, and took a deep breath. Then he stepped over the railing and began the climb down.

Hanging along the walls of the Red Castle, under the star-strewn night sky, looking out over dark forests stretching into the distance as far as he could see, it nearly seemed the past days had never even happened – as if he had never met that murderous bastard in the tavern downtown, never found himself thrown into a cell deep under the Red Castle, never fucked a queen in her own study. All those people barely even seemed to exist anymore, and very soon Tamar would no longer exist indeed. Very soon he would get out of this castle and return home and hopefully convince the Empress that all had happened exactly as it should have.

He found the railing of Tamar's small balcony beneath his feet and jumped the last yard down. Kneeling on the cold stones, he once more checked his knife, then stood up. The curtains were closed, but he could see the light of the fire dancing behind. She wasn't sleeping yet.

For the first time that night his nervousness stirred. If she was awake, he'd have to look her in the eyes again. She'd know she was about to die. Which of course she should have known since last night – and yet...

Runo closed his eyes and inhaled slowly, drawing the cool forest air deep into his lungs. Don't get attached. As simple as that. He had no reason to care, and all the reason not to. She would have ended up killing him too, had matters developed in a slightly different direction. Was he really going to endanger his own life for the wellbeing of just the next tyrant?

He opened the door before he could hesitate a moment longer.

Through the dark blue curtains. Into the fire-lit warmth of her room. His eyes found her bed first, and then the black-clad shape curled up in her blankets. Looking like she was asleep after all – except that she jolted up the moment his gaze fell on her.

For a moment he thought she was another woman entirely.

Her red hair loose and tangled. Her bewildered eyes shooting over his face and blade, her hands trembling.

Traces of tears on her pale cheeks, and a barely suppressed sob as she shrunk away from him in her blankets, grasping for her own knife between her skirts. She looked like a frightened little bird, a young girl lost in the dark woods – a transformation so jarring that he had to blink two, three times to be sure she was the same queen he'd found on that hardwood throne downstairs, the queen who had succumbed to his touches mere hours ago.

His knife hand sank down. He barely even noticed.

'What in the world is the matter with *you*?'

'Oh, for hell's sake.' She tried to snap, he could tell by the strained tone of her voice, but the words came falling out blurred by near-sobs, and her biting laugh sounded as much as a cry for help. 'You come falling into my room with a knife *again* and think I'll believe that you give a damn about whatever the matter is? You – you...'

She folded into her blankets, the last of her restraint crumbling – curled into a copper-haired, black-clad ball of furious blubbering. Runo stared at her. His feet seemed nailed to the floor, the knife suddenly twice as heavy in his hands. Do it now, he told himself. No sense in delaying the inevitable – she really won't forgive you if you excuse yourself more elaborately. But his body wouldn't move. He didn't manage to tear his eyes away from her bawling figure, looking less like a tyrannical monarch than anyone he'd ever had the displeasure of knowing in his life.

'Just *do* it, then!' she snarled, looking up with the tears running freely over her face. Her knife shook in her fist. 'If it really makes you feel better about yourself...'

He lurched forward and grabbed her by the bodice of her dress, fending off her desperate knife swing with his free arm. Her body felt too warm under his fingers, far too alive. She struggled against his hold when he pushed her down in the blankets, gasping for breath, powerless – too much like her writhing body under his hands that afternoon. His arousal stirred, and wouldn't stop stirring even when he pressed the flat side of his blade against her pale throat. Tamar froze as soon as the metal touched her skin, drew in a trembling breath.

'So much for my leniency, then, Taavi?'

'Don't,' he hissed. He should just finish this now – why hadn't he yet? 'We both know leniency has no part to play in this game. You'd have killed me if you—'

'I swore I wouldn't, damn you!'

'You can swear whatever you want – you'd be mad to keep me alive.'

'For hell's sake,' she spat, her face contorted into a twisted grimace, 'what do you think I *am*? That bloody Empress of yours?'

He froze for a fraction too long. 'What?'

'Think I'm going around making empty promises all day? That I take pleasure in tying nooses around as many necks as possible?' She sucked in another breath, her throat rising against the pressure of his knife. 'I *mean* these things when I say them. I'm not killing you.

I gave you my word and I damn well intend to keep it – so tell me again how we're playing the same game?'

Runo stared at her. A twitch of his hand, a turn of his wrist, and she'd be a bleeding corpse at his feet.

He didn't move.

'You have no reason to keep me alive in any game,' he said – pleading, nearly, although he didn't know for what. 'I know your kind. You'd never take the risk of—'

'My *kind*? What is my kind, according to you?'

He wanted to laugh, but his chuckle came out joyless as a grinning skull. 'The bloody kind of power-hungry tyrants who insist on—'

'A power-hungry tyrant? You call *me* the power-hungry tyrant in this fight?'

'Have you seen yourself?'

'Oh, you think I *want* this power?' she bit out. Her voice grew explosively louder in the half-dark silence of her dying fire. 'You think I *wanted* to be queen of this rat's nest when some bastard shot an arrow into my father's face? That I *want* to deal with all of them, the lords starving their people and the petty disputes taking dozens of commoners' lives and the bastard who wouldn't stop luring farmers' daughters into his bed? Do I really look like this is the life I was dreaming of when I was sixteen and stupid?'

'You—'

'So what else would you have me do, then?' she snapped. 'Continue to ignore it like my father did? Convince myself that the crooks and frauds are doing what's best for their people and stuff myself with food in my pretty castle until one of them kills me too? Those are *my* people out there suffering and dying, do you understand? *Someone* has to give a damn about them, and who's going to do it if not me?'

Runo stared at her. A hazel-brown fire burnt in her eyes, something so passionate it came close to fury – a dangerous, dazzling rage, the kind that would kill her before it died itself.

'So this is what I became,' she continued, her voice hoarse under his blade. 'This is what I made myself – someone they can't deceive, someone they can't hurt, someone they can't dazzle their way around. Because they'll kill each other if they can, and take all of the kingdom with them – because *someone* needs to protect them. Now tell me again I'm doing this for the joy of it, will you? Tell me just how much I love this bloody crown?'

Runo's fingers cramped around the hilt of his knife. His heart pulsed at his temples, a feeling that seemed to be half shame and half something else, something he felt so rarely he had trouble naming it – something that left him lost for words for a few frightening moments. Fierce, defiant brown eyes stared back at him, the fire of her fury nowhere near quenched by the tears still running over her face – and it was in that moment that he knew he couldn't do it. Not now. Not like this. Not if he didn't want to see that look haunting him in his dreams for the rest of his life.

He loosened his hand from her bodice with stiff, uneasy movements, pulled back his knife and sank down in the blankets at her feet. Tamar followed him with wary eyes, unmoving in the place where he'd held her pressed down.

Her kind. Had he ever seen the Empress give a damn about a single commoner's life ruined by her policies?

'You...' he started again.

Then he didn't know how to continue. Behind him, the fire crackled, a strangely homely sound for flames that had witnessed the near murder of a queen. Tamar's raging breath was the only other sound that broke the deep silence of this warm room, with its heavy velvet curtains and its golden wooden floor and the bed on which she had overpowered him a night ago. The bed where she was now sitting, two feet away from him, tear-stained and rumpled, and staring at him as if he were a crossbow about to fire.

'I?' she eventually said.

'Soldiers were looking for me. I heard them. If they'd found me...'

'I told them to keep you alive.'

He managed a laugh. 'Why *would* you?'

'Gave you my word.'

Runo opened his mouth, closed it again. And why would she care about whatever word she gave to a man out to kill her? To keep up appearances to her court? Then why didn't she just tell one of her guards to kill him in secret and claim she never knew about the plan?

What do you think I am?

With a curse he jolted up and flung his knife into the room. It smacked against the white wall on the other side and clattered to the floor, far out of his reach. Still Tamar didn't move, except for her eyes following his every move as he pulled his legs onto her bed and turned back to her. She held his gaze for a few more moments, more defiant with every next heartbeat, until she abruptly averted her face.

'Why are you doing this to me?'

'What – not killing you?'

'Oh, piss off.' A cheerless laugh. 'Killing me, not killing me. Stripping me naked. Pretending you care, then killing me again. What's the next step? Are you going to treat me to some life advice before you draw that knife at me again?'

Runo closed his eyes. For the bloody gods' sake – *he* didn't even know what the next step was. 'Are you looking for life advice?'

'Piss *off*.'

He managed a grin. 'You do look like you could use some, truth be told.'

'You...' She bit out another laugh that could have frozen burning oil. 'Hell's sake, you're just toying around with me after all, aren't you?'

Don't toy with me... He could still hear her say it, breathless and dazed with lust. The memory flickered through his loins with more enthusiasm than he needed right now, faced with the rage in her eyes and that nameless, unsettling feeling still quickening his heartbeat.

'Does it make a difference to you?' he said.

'If my life is a joke to you? That's supposed to leave me indifferent?'

'Oh, but that's not the issue, is it?' He smiled, ignoring the furious lines on her face. A damn suicidal idea, presumably, to be so attracted to that murderous spark in her eyes – but gods help him, she *was* beautiful, in a fierce, ruthless way he had never expected below the heartless façade. 'Your problem is you can't predict me. Hard to control me if you don't know in what direction I'll be going next, hm?'

'Oh, go to hell,' she snapped. 'You don't get to tell me what my problems are after you pressed a knife to my throat. If you were still hoping for me to believe you cared a whit about my problems, you've quite ruined your own chances by now.'

Runo shrugged. 'You don't think I might tell you something sensible even if I don't give a damn?'

'I don't need your sensible opinions, thank you very much.'

'You're a very bad liar, Tamar.'

She stiffened. 'And don't call me...'

'By your name? You'd rather go by Her Majesty, Queen Tamar of Redwood at all times?' He gave her a wry grin. 'No miracle you're dying of loneliness.'

'I'm *not*—'

'Liar.'

'Stop it!' she burst out, like a fire flaring up, with a wild, uncontrolled gesture at him. 'You have no right – no reason – why are you even still here? To laugh at me? To tell me I'm pathetic and pitiable and then kill me anyway? Might as well slit my throat immediately, if that's—'

'There's nothing pathetic about you, Tamar. Don't be ridiculous.'

She fell silent, staring at him with heaving breath and shaking hands. Runo looked away. He should be leaving, he knew. He should have left already. But she was so beautiful, and so lost, and he didn't want her to glare at him with so much disgust after the intoxicated look she'd given him this afternoon.

'There's something in between pathetic and invulnerable, do you realise that?' He spoke to the floorboards, or at least to anything other than that look in her eyes – but somehow he could still feel her gaze piercing through him. 'It's not pathetic to ask for help rather than demand it. It's not pathetic to *feel* something every now and then, or to doubt, or to admit a mistake. But you've been so busy making people fear and respect you that you never allowed them to love you – and that's catching up with you now, isn't it?'

She stayed silent. He sank back against her footboard and groaned.

'That's the trouble if you eliminate every unpleasant surprise in your life. You're suppressing every pleasant surprise as well. Every spontaneous gesture. And commanding people to care for you doesn't work terribly well, I suppose.'

Tamar was staring at him when he looked up. Her lips had parted a fraction, her eyes opened too wide. No trace of iron left on her – just a frightened, desperate woman, looking ten years younger than the queen he'd thought he would kill, and ten times more human. She met his gaze for only a moment, then closed her eyes and wiped the tangled red locks from her face.

'Any more wisdom to offer?'

Her voice sounded flatter, the hard edge of it gone. Runo shrugged, to convince himself more than to convince her.

'As a general piece of advice, don't expect assassins to care about your wellbeing.'

'I didn't—'

'Sure you didn't.'

'I'm not an *idiot*, Taavi.'

'You're damn well desperate enough to behave like one, then.'

'You...'

The words never found their way to her lips. She sat wrestling with them in silence for a moment, her eyes on his face, her shoulders sagged. Then she looked away and muttered, 'I should have you hanged for saying this alone.'

'Do you hear yourself? And then you're surprised when I end up believing you're some power-hungry tyrant?'

Tamar scoffed. 'You're working for the wrong person if you have that much of a problem with power-hungry tyrants.'

'No need to tell me,' he said sourly. 'Why do you think that iron act of yours gets on my nerves so much?'

'Then why in the world *are* you...'

Her sentence died away without a conclusion, but her expression didn't soften – a sharp, inquisitive frown, her eyes scanning his face for some hint, some clue on the answer. Runo felt the grin slip off his face under that look like water slipping off waxed cloth. Why in the world was he working for the Empress? An easy question, a question for perhaps the only truth he had ever held as a given in his life – but with those hazel eyes on his face, far too earnest in their interest, he couldn't think of the right answer for a single, blood-curdling heartbeat.

'Why would you care?' he said.

It came out too curt. Tamar leaned closer, her red locks falling over her shoulders as she tilted her head.

'Ah, you're the only one here allowed to dig around in the minds of others?'

Runo held her gaze, unable to move. Her look was an invitation, and one that came with far too much temptation – but he should know better, he really should. It didn't matter that this quiet, closed room seemed barely connected to the bitter world outside anymore, that it felt like this conversation would forever stay between these four walls. It didn't matter that she had looked at him with what was nearly awe this afternoon, a look nobody should be giving assassins who only lived to survive. He couldn't get attached. He'd leave. He'd still have to kill her.

'Come on,' she said, a small smile playing around her lips. Lips he had kissed. Why did the memory of their sweet taste return so violently to him now? 'An answer for an answer. Still not a ridiculous demand, is it?'

His laughter rose in him like the tide, and suddenly he knew the name of that feeling itching in his chest – admiration. For hell's sake. He'd fucked her on her own desk, escaped her cells, pressed a knife to her throat, and she still had the guts to *joke* with him?

It shouldn't matter. He wasn't supposed to talk about this – a story he had locked away with the last breaths of his victims, secrets too dark to speak about. But here he was, sitting on the bed of the queen of Redwood herself, the air around her heavy with words she should never have spoken out loud to him, and somehow he didn't think she would scoff at him. He'd seen that vehement, nearly violent loyalty that lay behind what he'd taken for a simple lust for power. Even the empty eyes staring at him from the back of his thoughts couldn't shake that image off his mind.

An answer for an answer. Oh, hell, why not.

'She saved my life,' he said. 'The Empress.'

Tamar raised an eyebrow. 'Unusual.'

'I'm an exceptional man in many ways,' he said, and she bit her lip in a meagre attempt to suppress a chuckle.

'I see. Go on, then, Taavi.'

'Not a Taavi, technically speaking. Was born in Cuvri.'

At once the amusement evaporated from her face. '*Cuvri*? You...'

Her sentence died away, but he could read the question in her eyes – why in the world are you working for the woman who spent decades waging war on the clans of your homeland? She was visibly making an effort to choose her words carefully as she slowly said, 'The war – did you get caught up in it?'

'Not in the Taavi war, originally. Internal struggles, first.' He hesitated, then continued, 'The village where I was born – it wasn't big, but it controlled the entrance to some strategic valley. It became the target of some civil war when I was seven. Our elders swore fealty to one clan chieftain, another few of them took offence, you know how it goes. They laid siege to the place for weeks.'

'Oh, gods. Did you still have food?'

'Less and less of it.'

She closed her eyes for a moment, her lips a thin line.

'I know,' Runo said, his voice too flat. 'People started starving pretty damn quickly. But after a few weeks we received news that the warring clans had closed some deal, that we were getting a few bags of grain again, some fruit and vegetables...'

He swallowed. Tamar didn't interrupt him.

'I had grown ill by that point. They didn't dare to let me eat bread yet, were afraid it would kill me. So they brought me berries in bed and left me there while they went to bake their bread on the market square, all of them together, making sure it was equally distributed.'

He didn't want to continue. He didn't want to bring the words over his lips, make it happen all over again. But they were out before he could stop himself –

'Turned out the grain was poisoned.'

The fire still crackled in the silence that followed, but Tamar's breath caught. When he looked up, there was a suspicious gleam in her brown eyes, a look as if she might lean over and hug him any moment.

'My mother...' He looked away. 'She tried to warn me. Came falling into our hut, gabbling that I shouldn't eat any of the bread. Then died before my eyes. I went out. Found the rest of them – dozens of them. Everyone I'd ever known. Sitting around that table, lying around the square. Dead.'

'Did anyone else...'

'One newborn girl who died the next day. Apart from her – just me.'

He heard her shift in the blankets and didn't dare to look up. For all he knew he'd break down and fall into her arms if he met her eyes again.

'And you said...' She hesitated. 'Those rivalling chieftains were the ones who poisoned the grain?'

He nodded.

'I think I read something about it,' she said, and again she wavered for a moment. 'Or a similar case – I don't remember the details. I don't think the books mentioned any survivors.'

'Why would they?' he said bitterly. 'I never committed any grand deeds of revenge, never saved a single life. I just walked around the same ghost village for a week, living off vegetable scraps. Couldn't think of anywhere else to go.'

'While they were still – there.'

'The corpses. Yes.'

He saw them again now, following him with their empty eyes from the shadowy corners of this half-dark room. A faint memory of the stench found his nostrils, dead flesh in the scorching summer sun, following him into every street, every hut...

'How did you get out?' Tamar said quietly.

'A Taavi army heard of the massacre, pulled the warring parties apart, came to check how much of it was true. Brought me to Raulinna to tell the Empress herself whatever I knew about the conflict – which wasn't much, really. The man who took me captive intended to kill me as soon as I'd served my purpose. The Empress...'

In the back of his mind, he could still hear her voice, could still feel the flood of relief soothing weeks of nauseating fear. *The child played no part in this war yet. He may serve us and live.*

Tamar sighed before he could finish his sentence. 'I see.'

'Do you?'

Perhaps he sounded too sceptical; this time she was the one to pause. Only after a long few heartbeats did she say, 'You've met Amiran.'

Runo grimaced. 'To our mutual enjoyment.'

'Yes, thank you,' she said with a sour grin. 'His father tried to kill mine when I was five years old or so. People found out about the plot. My uncle was sentenced to death. Most of the court wanted to have Amiran executed too – he was a child, but the son of a traitor, you know the argument.'

'Your father refused to kill him?'

She nodded. 'I don't think a day goes by in which he doesn't think about it. He'd have done anything for my father. It's one of the reasons I trust him more than anyone else in Redwood. So yes – I think I do understand.'

Runo averted his eyes, feeling unfathomably relieved for reasons he couldn't quite figure out. 'Thanks.'

Again they were silent for a few moments.

'Did you stay in Raulinna?' she said. 'After they brought you there?'

'They tried to make a soldier out of me first.' He scratched the back of his head, coughed. 'That didn't work out particularly well. Turns out that armies want you to – well...'

Tamar sniggered. 'To follow instructions every now and then?'

Runo looked up. She was wrestling down a grin, and gave up the fight the moment their eyes met; the laughter escaped them simultaneously, a shared chuckle of a strange, unexpected relief, a sudden harmony. Something relaxed in his shoulders. On the other side of the bed Tamar slid half a foot down in her pillows and wrapped her arms around herself, her wry smile lingering on her face.

'So you switched professions?'

'It's just...' What was the worst she could do – call him a monster? 'It doesn't disgust me like most people. Killing. I lived with the dead for a week. I got used to them. If anything...'

Tamar tilted her head when he stayed silent. He rubbed a hand over his face.

'There's something comforting about the sight of dead eyes, if you want to know. It reminds me of home, I suppose.'

'Yes,' she said quietly.

'So.' He shrugged his most insincere shrug. 'I kill people, and I survive, and that's enough of a life for me. Does that answer your question?'

She was silent for so long that he looked up eventually, bracing himself for a look of disgust, of scorn, of ridicule. But she sat staring at him in the pillows, her lips a tight pink line, her gaze softer than he had ever seen it before. As their eyes met, her hand came up half an inch, then fell down again.

'Hm?' he said

"*Is* it enough of a life?'

'What else would I want?' he said, looking away. 'Some great ideal to believe in? Principles are terribly unhelpful things in Raulinna, and frankly, they've always seemed a little boring to me.'

She sighed. 'I suppose you have friends at home?'

'None who wouldn't betray me to save their own life,' he said curtly. 'Which is fine. It's mutual.'

'Well. Relationships?'

He gave her a rather suggestive look – he couldn't help it. Relationships. Gods be damned, why did she have to look so much like the woman who set her nails into his back to keep him inside her mere hours ago?

'You think this is how I'd treat you if I had a wife waiting for me?'

She blushed. Gods help him, the Iron Queen of Redwood *blushed*. Desperately ignoring the sudden rush of blood into his loins, he added, 'Not my particular kind of dishonour, for all the kinds I do admittedly dabble in. There's nothing meaningful going on at home.'

'Good to know,' she said, a little too pensive. That definitely didn't send his blood flowing in any more sensible directions. 'Where did you learn the language?'

He blinked. 'Beg your pardon?'

'My language,' she repeated, keeping her eyes on his face with a sharpness that suggested she at least suspected where she was sending his memories. 'You speak it surprisingly fluently. Have you been to Redwood before?'

'Oh.' He wanted to lie for a moment, desperately so – but lying didn't make sense. It would suggest the memory bothered him. That he *had* felt too much about it, all those years ago. 'No, this is my first time in this part of the world. I knew a girl from here once, she taught me most of it.'

'Knew a girl.' The suggestion was shamelessly obvious. 'Your vocabulary is quite developed in certain... departments.'

Runo bit out a laugh. 'What are you trying to get from me?'

'If you learned an entire language for her, it doesn't sound that meaningless to me.'

'She's dead,' he said brusquely. 'Leave it be. It was fun once, and then it ended. It didn't matter – it still doesn't matter. I didn't care much about her.'

Tamar raised an eyebrow. 'You don't care much about anyone, if I'm understanding all of this correctly.'

'I did once. Then it died on me. And in a place like Raulinna, it's easier to live if you don't have much to lose.' He glanced at her, reading the next question on her face. 'So no, don't expect me to care about your wellbeing. But if it's anything of a consolation, you're better company than I expected.'

'Trying to flatter me again, aren't you?' she said.

Runo burst out laughing. She looked away, shaking her head but unable to suppress her grin, and muttered, 'You really are impossible.'

He shrugged. 'So are you.'

'Admittedly.' She sank sideways in her pillows and pulled up her knees like a little girl about to fall asleep. 'Glad we sorted that out.'

He chuckled. Then neither of them spoke. It was a silence that wrapped itself around Runo's shoulders like a soft, warm cloak and left him feeling so comfortable it was nearly drowsy – that uncanny cosiness of shared secrets, them against the rest of the world. Which it wasn't – it was them against each other, of course he knew better – but couldn't he forget about that small detail until sunrise? Hell's sake, he wanted to lie down and wrap his arms around her. He wanted to run his fingers through her hair and feel her hands on his back again and hold her, just feel the warmth and

146

strength and safety of her and fall asleep against her in the snugness of these blankets.

Although he wouldn't be averse to some more advanced activities either.

He closed his eyes, leaning back until the hard edge of the wooden footboard cut into his shoulder blades. His breath grew thinner in his lungs. He couldn't touch her. Not again. He remembered his confusion in his cell, mere hours ago – if he allowed her to get that close to him again, he might grow a little too attached after all...

'Runo?' she muttered.

He froze, looking up. She hadn't raised her head from the pillow, or even opened her eyes; for a moment he thought she was already sleeping and his name had fallen from her lips in some hazy, drowsy dream. His *name*.

'Hm?' he managed.

'Just...' Her voice sounded small in all its sleepiness. 'Thanks for saying these things. I think I needed to hear them.'

Something tugged at his heart, an elation so violent it hurt. He hesitated, then leaned forward. She still didn't open her eyes.

'Thanks for listening, too.'

A small smile perked up the corners of her lips. 'You're very welcome.'

He averted his eyes from her peaceful beauty, clenching his jaws. No. No, he couldn't touch her. He couldn't kiss her. He *definitely* couldn't strip her dress off her shoulders and tuck her into bed, naked and beautiful and willing in his arms – but gods be damned, why did she have to look so *human*?

'I should be going,' he forced himself to say, and she made a soft sound that could indicate disappointment as easily as agreement. When he turned back to her, she still hadn't moved.

'Will see you again,' he added. 'Soon, probably.'

That quiet smile again. 'Is that a threat?'

And then his hand moved anyway, before he could stop it – stroked over forehead, brushed a red lock off her cheeks, came to a rest around the back of her head. Still Tamar didn't move, but her breath quickened under his touches.

'Look at me,' he said softly.

For a single heartbeat the world remained motionless. Then she blinked open her eyes and met his gaze with a mixture of quiet vulnerability and fear and something that looked nearly like *trust*, something that sent a twisting jolt of nervousness through his guts.

He leaned towards her, slowly, and she didn't shrink back.

He had to stop himself. He knew he had to stop himself. But she was barely ten inches away from him – five – two – close enough to feel her breath on his face...

Their lips met before he could drag himself back. A single feathery kiss – a reassurance, or an apology, or even a promise, although he had no idea what for. A shiver ran through her under his fingers, and somehow he felt that more sharply than even his own pounding heart.

'Sleep well,' he whispered. 'I'll see you soon.'

He did not look back as he stood, picked up his knife off the floor again, stepped out onto the balcony, and began the climb up through Redwood's silent winter night. If he looked back, he wasn't sure he would ever leave at all.

CHAPTER 10

T amar did sleep well.

She slept so well, even, that she didn't wake until the vigorous knocking on her bedroom door eventually forced her to – long after sunrise, even in the middle of winter. But despite that forceful start of her morning, despite the fact she had fallen asleep in her stiff day dress, despite the disconcerting mess of memories of the past night, she woke with her mind calm and clear, a serenity that could not even be broken by the thought of the world waiting outside.

She was alive. She was *still* alive. And the assassin – Runo...

With a groan she sat up on the edge of her bed and scanned her room. No trace of him. As if he never walked in through her balcony doors, pushed a knife to her throat, told her about his Cuvri village, and...

She raised a hand to her mouth, cautiously pressed her fingertips against her lips. Had he *kissed* her?

Had she let him?

Only then did she realise that the steady beat of knuckles against her door still continued, with irregular intervals. She muttered a curse and got up, brushed the worst wrinkles from her skirts, and steeled herself. Whatever was going on, if it required minutes of knocking, she shouldn't ignore it for a daydream. Even if it was a daydream of the man who should have killed her last night –

And hadn't?

For hell's sake – a question for later.

She ran a hand through her hair in the few steps to the other side of her room, just enough to tame the worst of the chaos, and unlocked the door. When she swung it open, she found Amiran on her doorstep, flustered and rumpled, surrounded by a handful of guards.

'Thank the gods, Tamar, I nearly started thinking...'

Only then did it occur to her that he would have stood here knocking for a far, far longer time if Runo hadn't so abruptly changed his mind last night. A shiver ran over her back.

'Apologies,' she said, and it didn't come out as confident as usual. 'I was fast asleep, it seems – is there anything wrong?'

'Some news about the assassin.'

Her blood turned cold. 'What is it?'

'One of Reziko's informants heard some rumour downtown,' Amiran said, and every muscle in her chest relaxed at once – rumours downtown. Not some overly zealous guard piercing a sword through him at first sight, then. 'It seems that over the course of this night someone closed a deal with some unseemly fellows from Woodside District. About your assassin. About his life, that is.'

Tamar stared at him, her shoulders tensing up again. 'Gods' sake. How much?'

'Fifty pieces of gold.'

"*Fifty*?'

'Exactly.' He grimaced. 'Someone seems quite determined not to let him escape.'

'Good gods,' she said, blinking. Fifty pieces of gold. A melodious voice still echoing in her ears, soft lips on hers. 'I doubt it's about his escape. More about what he might tell us if we found him first – but hell, that's a lot of gold to put on anyone's head.'

'No half measures.'

'No. Who even *has* that kind of money, apart from...'

Amiran threw a glance over his shoulder, at the empty corridor behind him. 'Apart from the nobles around the castle?'

'Yes.'

'Or it could be a bluff,' he said slowly. 'I'll admit, promising some Woodside District bastard a cartload of gold without delivering the prize sounds like a risky kind of undertaking – but he might be desperate.'

She closed her eyes for a fraction of a moment. Desperate. To silence Runo before he could tell her more about the man who hired him – but he didn't *know* who hired him. He'd told her he knew as little as she did. Why would her traitor go to such lengths to protect his identity if he had already hidden himself so well?

'I suppose that goes to show he should indeed know more,' she managed. 'The assassin.'

Amiran looked decidedly unhappy. 'You still want us to keep him alive?'

'Yes.'

Had she spoken too quickly? He gave her a concerned frown, then turned to one of their guards and said, 'Let Terenti know, will you?'

The man nodded and hurried off. Amiran turned back to her, giving her another uncomfortably suspicious glance.

'Can I come in?'

Tamar stepped back without an answer, and he closed the door behind him as he followed her into the room. His frown didn't soften.

'What is it?' she said, a sudden nervousness twisting through her. He still knew her far too well. If he had only the slightest suspicion of the war waging in her head...

'Tamar.' He cleared his throat. 'Is there anything you're not telling me about the bastard? Because you seem...'

She waited. He hesitated again, then gave a frustrated gesture. 'You seem a little off about him.'

'Off?' she said.

A worthless answer, but she had to say *something*, and what other options did she have? Oh, yes, to tell you the truth, he fucked me into blissful ecstasy and made me feel more alive than I've felt in years, told me things I never understood about myself and kissed me goodnight, and now he's still out to kill me. I'm more confused than I've been in all my life – can I please just be a little *off* about him in peace?

'He's toying with you,' Amiran said, slowly, thinking every word through before it left his lips. 'He was when we stood there at his cell, at least. Trying to provoke you, to get under your skin – you're not letting him, are you?'

I'm not toying at all...

'No – no, of course, I know better.'

He still didn't look away from her. 'Are you sure?'

'Do I look unsure?'

'Taavi are too good at these games, Tamar. You shouldn't—'

'He's Cuvrian,' she blurted out, nearly a reflex, and Amiran's eyes narrowed.

'How do you know?'

'Oh, he – he mentioned something about it.'

'Something?'

She hesitated a fraction too long. Something. The whole gruelling story, the glimpses of the darkness in his eyes. She'd seen it in his face even while he wouldn't meet her gaze: somewhere in his mind that frightened, numbed seven-year-old boy was still living in a hill village full of corpses. The poisoned city – she *had* heard the story before, but the details...

'Tamar?'

'Apologies.' She forced a smile. 'Just thinking. Speaking of Cuvri, could you walk by the archives and ask them to bring me the chronicles of the Cuvri War around – say, twenty-five years ago? Some little things I'd like to check.'

Amiran didn't move. 'He *is* getting under your skin, isn't he, Tamar?'

'Don't worry about it.'

'Tamar—'

'Look,' she interrupted, too sharply, 'I don't want to die either, remember? I'm not doing anything stupid. That's all you need to know.'

She knew the expression that twisted over his face, and was too late; before she could say anything, soften the worst of the blow, he stepped back and snapped, 'In that case, feel free to handle Terenti's nagging about the Tanglewood case yourself. Can't really take that over if I don't know shit, can I?'

'Sure,' she said with a bitter laugh. 'I'll just...'

But he stalked off before she could finish that sentence, throwing the door shut behind him with a bang loud enough to shake the glass on her nightstand.

Terenti sat waiting for her in her study when she finally gathered the courage to face the world again. At the sight of him she nearly turned back around to lock herself in her bedroom – what if he *was* the person who let Runo into the castle? What if he decided, after two unfinished attempts at her life, that he ought to take matters into his own hands?

But he could also be innocent, and either way there was no sense in antagonising him even further.

'Morning,' she said, leaving the door open so that her guards could listen along. 'How's the search?'

She knew how the search was doing, but the reminder of a disappointing performance couldn't hurt to weaken his case. Unless...

Her heart cramped. If he was the person behind all this madness, the person who had shot those arrows into Runo's cell a night ago, would he even tell her if they found him? Or would he, quickly and with characteristic efficiency, smuggle his corpse out of the castle and conclude after two days of searching that the assassin must have fled and escaped?

Oh, gods. She should have found someone else to coordinate this search. She should have thought of it yesterday.

'I don't doubt we'll find him within mere hours,' Terenti said, interrupting her flare of panic with the usual distant determination – so different from his brother's hot-headedness, in a way that didn't seem to fit his bulldog-like features. 'He'll have to sleep eventually. He can't keep moving forever. My men are taking care of it.'

'And it is very clear that I want him alive, isn't it?'

'Incomprehensible, but clear.' His voice had turned another step colder. 'We're doing all we can. My men have been instructed.'

'And you're making sure he's not leaving the castle either?'

'Obviously, Tamar.'

'Good. Glad to hear.' She sank into her chair and took a deep breath in some attempt to calm her hammering heart. At least if he didn't find Runo soon she'd have an excuse to put someone else on the case – and the assassin wouldn't allow himself to be killed too quietly in some dusty corner of the castle, would he? *Someone* would notice a fight?

'Very welcome,' Terenti said – the politest and most obvious of lies. 'Could we have a word on Rusuvan, then?'

For hell's sake. She *should* have asked Amiran to handle this – but she knew her cousin, and after his outburst of this morning it would take at least two days and a damn good bottle of wine before he would grant her any such favours again.

'I didn't hear from Tanglewood yet,' she said, turning away to order the documents on her desk. Letters she still had to read, contracts she still had to sign. 'I'm not sure what you expect me to say today that I haven't already said.'

'You do realise that the longer you hesitate about this, the more people will doubt your...'

'There would be no reason to hesitate,' Tamar said between clenched teeth, 'if you hadn't been harassing me every free minute with your attempts to change my mind. I believe I have always been clear about my preferences.'

'And this is what you call a fair trial, Tamar?' A sharp chuckle. 'When you've known from the beginning where you wanted to have the poor fellow?'

Yes, she wanted to snap, I have known where I wanted him from the beginning indeed – in front of a number of capable judges who know the law, know the facts, and have no reason to favour him. In a fair trial. Now get out of my room before I *make* you leave, and be happy we leave the matter at that.

In the back of her mind she heard Runo laugh again, his honeyed, strangely persuasive voice. *Do you hear yourself? And then you're surprised when I end up believing you're some power-hungry tyrant?*

Oh, for hell's sake. Did she hear herself? *So busy making people fear and respect you...*

And then what was she supposed to do now?

She drew in a deep breath. Her fingers were trembling in her lap all of a sudden. She might be wrong, she sternly reminded herself. Terenti might not be the person trying to kill her. Perhaps the worst of his offences was nagging for days about a court case his old friend brought upon himself. But even then –

No shame in asking for help.

'Tamar?'

She closed her eyes for the shortest moment. If this goes wrong, she told the golden eyes staring at her from her memory, if this kills me, I'll damn well know who to blame.

'Tell me, then,' she said, sagging back in her chair and turning to look at the chainmail-clad man still sitting in her windowsill. 'What would you advise me to do?'

Terenti blinked, a moment of frozen astonishment that would have been amusing if not for the fright raging through her, the sense of control slipping through her fingers.

'Beg your pardon?'

'What would you advise me to do?' she repeated, slower now. 'In the Tanglewood case.'

He frowned. 'You already know what I'm asking you to do – I don't see...'

'No, no, you misunderstand me. I'm not asking what you want me to do, I'm asking you what you think would be wisest if you were in my seat. I'm...' She managed a smile. Her fingers were still trembling. 'I'm asking for your help, Terenti.'

If she had told him she planned to invade the Taavi Empire with three soldiers and a single horse, he couldn't have looked more bewildered. 'What?'

'Help. You know the concept, don't you?'

'I – Tamar, are you alright?'

'Oh, perfectly fine.' Another smile she didn't feel. They came easier with practice. 'But I'm a little lost with this particular case. And you seem to be an expert on the matter by now, so I thought I might as well ask what you would do in my place.'

'What I...'

He came up from the windowsill with a baffled chuckle and paced five steps into the room. Then, turning on his heels, he said, 'I meant what I said about trying to spare you the headache, Tamar. In your place, I'd want to make sure not to antagonise some of my most powerful dukes, frankly. Don't see why a couple of lost pieces of silver would be worth that risk.'

'Yes, but you know it's not just about the silver, don't you?'

He opened his mouth, paused, then said, 'Could you elaborate?'

'For example,' Tamar said, 'you've been complaining to me about what's-her-name of Old Arches – Makvala, isn't it? You've been complaining about her mismanagement of her mother's gold, and presumably rightly so, if it's escalating to the extent that it leaves that part of the border unprotected. We're looking into that. Might officially sue her somewhere in the following months. People – powerful people – will be bothering me to put her on a Lord's Trial as well. And you know *she* has friends who'll acquit her without second thought.'

Terenti stared at her with narrowed eyes, his lips twisted in a bitter smirk.

'I don't know how I should refuse them if I just granted another man the same favour in similar circumstances, Terenti. So if you have any suggestions – please let me know. But I really don't see how to separate these cases.'

'You...' He hesitated again, his frown deepening. 'Well, at least Rusuvan's slight oversights never threatened international relations.'

'His village representatives wrote me about farmers desperate enough to smuggle their cows into Copper Coast fields to prevent them from being taken as tax payments. If Ulrick had heard, I doubt he'd have been amused.'

'Yes, but...'

'And even if we find a formal difference between Rusuvan and Makvala – a difference that doesn't hinge on the question of whether they're guilty, because I'm not assuming anything on that question yet – even if we find a formal difference here, what tells me we won't have some similar case in five years? Ten? Some case where we'll both want to make sure the subjects aren't—'

'Yes,' he interrupted. 'Yes, I hear what you're saying, Tamar – yes, that is of course an issue we should take into account – but I'd still advise you...'

His sentence died away. Would still advise her to leave Rusuvan to his old friends – but how could he defend that suggestion now that he was suddenly supposed to be the authority here?

A last moment of silence; then he abruptly turned away from her and muttered a curse. 'I'll think about this.' Even that sounded like a curse. 'Will let you know.'

'I'm very grateful in advance.'

He grumbled some answer she didn't understand, threw her a last befuddled glance, and strode out without closing the door behind him.

It – worked?

It *worked*?

Tamar stood up from her desk, a little wobbly on her feet. She walked over to the door and pretended not to notice her guards' looks of confusion as she shut it. She leaned back against the wood and sucked in a deep breath in the sudden, blissful silence, and another breath, until the air in her lungs felt cool and clean and utterly relieved.

And then she could no longer suppress her laugh, sinking through her knees with her back against the door and her hand clutched over her mouth – an astounded, alleviated burst of laughter that left her with shaking hands and tears in her eyes.

CHAPTER 11

T he trumpet signalling a guard change woke Runo in the early morning as he lay wrapped in his blankets, on a thin reed mat that protected him from the cold stone of the balcony. The starry sky was still ink black above him, although the first hints of daylight came sneaking over the horizon to the east, a pale indigo that would soon turn a golden red. Yet the forest surrounding the Red Castle was still an impenetrable sea of black, and only the faint glow of some lights down the hill betrayed the location of the town where he had met the masked traitor three nights ago.

Runo groaned. Three nights? It seemed an eternity.

Under the cover of darkness he sat up from his improvised bed and stretched his stiff limbs until he felt the blood flow in his feet and fingers again. Then he wrapped his blankets around himself again and leaned back against the locked balcony doors, breathing warmth into his palms as he stared at the bare woods stretching out into the distance. The night wasn't as cold as the Cuvri winters in this land closer to the sea – but still cold enough, and significantly colder than Tamar's bed would have been.

The air abruptly left his lungs. Gods be damned, Tamar.

In the crisp clarity of the night, it was hard to imagine what in the world had come over him last night, what madness made him abandon his plans and convinced him to spend an hour spilling his most unpleasant secrets instead. But he could hardly deny it *had* come over him. It was hard to deny that it was the second time, too – that as a matter of fact, he had never kept himself sane in her vicinity.

Worse – if he was entirely honest, he quite enjoyed the madness.

He muttered a curse and leaned back against the cold stone, tucking his hands between his blankets. This couldn't be right. This couldn't be true. Now, far away from her intoxicating influence again, he ought to know better – good gods, why would he even enjoy her company at all? She was nothing to him. A foreign queen, ruling some tiny backwater kingdom miles away from his home and hearth. Just a woman trying to save her own life, like every miserable bastard he'd killed in the Empress's name. A little more beautiful than his average victim, a little more decent, too – but he should know better than to be fooled by a pretty face and some alluring smiles, shouldn't he?

To the east, the sunrise set the clouds just above the horizon on fire, flaming shreds of red breaking through the colourless paleness of the sky beyond. Below his tower the castle grew busier, noisier, rattling wagons and whinnying horses and shouting men all mingling into a constant cacophony of life. Still it seemed very silent on his little balcony, hidden from the eyes of the world. Not the silence of plans growing in his mind – rather the silence of a complete and utter absence of plans.

Why was he still doubting what he had to do?

His orders were clear. *Kill her, Runo. Kill the Iron Queen.* That assignment wouldn't change, even if he spent five more hours sitting here and staring into nothingness – Tamar had to die, simple as that. The only question ought to be *how* he would achieve that, not *if* it was going to happen.

He didn't even notice the sun had risen above the horizon until the golden rays found his face and his shoulders relaxed in the sudden warmth. Before him, the dewy branches of the forest glittered in the sunlight, transforming the bare trees into icy sculptures as far as the eye could see. A damn beautiful place, this kingdom – but then again, it wasn't *home*.

Finally some sharp lines emerged from the mist in his head again. Home over beauty. This, at long last, made sense. Fine, Tamar may not be the person he'd believed her to be – too quick-witted, too human, too beautiful. But she wasn't home. She wasn't the woman who plucked him from a conflict that should have killed him, given him a place to sleep and a way to survive. The Empress had trusted him to do right, that dreary morning in the Glass Hall. Was he really going to break her trust because he had been stupid enough to step into Tamar's alluring traps a few times too often? Enjoyable traps, perhaps, but that didn't matter. None of this had ever been about his enjoyment.

Time to stop whining. Time to shove these impractical sentiments aside and start doing his job again, time to stop lingering on some sudden, ridiculous attachment. Raulinna taught him better.

But it still took him half an hour to come into motion, and even when he took up his knife and made his way back into the castle, the clarity didn't fully return to his mind.

'Hey!' a sharp voice behind him barked. 'You!'

Gods be damned.

The corridor had been empty behind him a moment ago, and silent enough to lure him from the deserted bedroom where he spent the last hour waiting for a chance to move. But the gruff voice sounded too close, barely thirty feet behind him, as if the bastard had jumped from the nearest doorway as soon as Runo started walking.

Not what he needed now. Couldn't the world behave in accordance with his plans for *once* during this mission?

'You there! Halt!'

Runo stood still and slowly turned his head as the other man stomped closer. Walking on wouldn't help him much – the bastard was shouting loud enough to alarm a dozen of his colleagues within a minute, and *that* would definitely sour the situation. Now there was just this one guard, a stocky fellow squinting at him from under his helmet like a man making the discovery of the century.

'So *here* you are.'

'So it seems,' Runo said, smiling his most amiable smile as he fully turned around and ambled closer, his mind racing. 'Even more astonishing, it appears we are *both* here. Quite the coincidence, wouldn't you say? Of all the places where I could have been – and all the places where you could have been...'

Fifteen feet away the guard came to a befuddled standstill, his frown deepening. 'What?'

'Time and place. Fascinating concepts to think about.' Twelve feet. Ten. 'Had you just walked by a single minute later – had I been a few steps faster – you might never even have known I was anywhere near. And look at us now! You might just be the one to—'

'Wait – hey,' the guard interrupted, staggering back and grabbing for his sword. 'Hey, don't—'

Runo leaped forward.

The fight was short and ugly and pleasantly effective; a few punches, a few nasty kicks, a sword clattering to the floor, and his knife lay against the guard's unshaven throat. The man froze with a choked grunt, panting so heavily that Runo could smell the morning's porridge on his breath.

'You – you *bastard*.'

'Runo for friends,' Runo said, with another insincere smile to hide the thoughts tumbling through his mind. He had to get the man out of the way – but how definitively? 'Let's get a little more privacy before any of your colleagues finds us here.'

The guard didn't struggle as Runo steered him back into the room where he had hidden for the past hour, but his breath quickened. The rapid inhalations of a man who expected each of them to be the last – and was he wrong? No reason to keep him alive. If anything, he'd have valuable information about Runo's last location by the time colleagues found him. Yesterday the thought of Tamar's wrath had been reason to spare the unconscious prison guard, but even that argument...

A sting of nervousness stirred. It may as well be an advantage now, a furious Tamar. At least if he had killed one of her men, he could be sure she wouldn't give him that look of oddly genuine sympathy anymore, and that should quickly cure him of the urge to drop his knife and have another chat with her next time they met. If he couldn't bring himself to hate her, at least he could make it easier by giving her a reason.

Through the doorway, two steps aside to get out of view for whoever might pass outside. Under his knife, the guard shook like a twig in the wind.

'You're not getting away with this, Taavi.' It sounded like a plea. 'They'll find you. They'll—'

'Wishing them good luck,' Runo said, tightening his grip on his knife. 'I'll be out of the castle in time. Anything else?'

'Won't help you.' A gruff, wheezing laugh. 'Someone put a price on your head in town. Get out of the Red Castle, run into their hands. One knife won't save you from—'

'Someone put a price on my head?'

'Heard that right.'

'How much?'

The guard snorted. 'Fifty pieces of gold.'

Runo yanked back his knife and pushed the other man away from him. The guard nearly stumbled, caught himself against the nearest wall and stayed there, panting and shaking. 'What—'

'To be clear,' Runo interrupted, his mind whirring. A price on his head. Fifty pieces of gold – *fifty*. A ridiculous fortune, the kind of money for which hundreds of thugs would gladly chase him to every edge of the world if need be. 'This money – it's not coming from your queen herself, is it?'

The guard jerked around, eyeing him with cautious scorn. 'Of course it's not.'

I gave you my word. He couldn't suppress an unreasonable breath of relief. 'Then how do you know about it?'

'Her Spymaster caught rumours downtown.' A teeth-baring grin. 'Story is making the rounds, you see. Enough people who'll be on your trail as soon as you...'

Runo turned away, squeezing his fingers around his knife hilt. Enough people on his trail, yes. Gods be damned, he should have known the Redwood traitor wouldn't stay idle while he was hiding – that with Tamar protecting his life, other measures would be taken to make sure he couldn't talk...

Talk about *what*? He didn't know the man's name. Didn't know his face or voice, didn't know his position in the Red Castle. And yet the bastard seemed convinced he was a danger, convinced enough to waste fifty pieces of gold just to silence him.

Shouldn't that mean he was indeed a danger, in ways he couldn't fully comprehend yet?

He stepped away from the guard and sank down on the edge of the room's rickety bed, barely registering the loud creaking of the wood. Why couldn't everything be simple for once? He should just be killing Tamar. But if he found his way to her now and finished his job, he would step out into the world with half a town at his ankles and very few resources to make it back home safely.

Which meant he would be an idiot to kill her now.

He shouldn't be so relieved at the thought, but a weight fell off his shoulders nonetheless – not the time to kill her. First he needed to get that damned traitor out of the way. When there was nobody left to pay the price on his head, when he would be able to leave the Red Castle again – by that time he could focus on killing Tamar.

In the meantime...

Well, she wanted the bastard dead as much as he did, didn't she?

He nearly laughed. Clearly he was going mad. But the idea welling up in him was too pleasant in too many ways, and even better, he might be able to justify it to the Empress too.

A movement in the corner of his eye shook him from his thoughts. The guard was sneaking closer to the door, towards the corridor, towards his sword. Runo coughed. The other froze.

'Question,' Runo said. 'You received an order not to kill me, yes?'

The guard scowled at him. 'How do you know?'

'Long story.' He sighed, gave his knife a last glance, then shrugged and flicked it onto the floor. Out of reach. Sometimes it was better to force your own decisions. 'You're very welcome, brother.'

'You – what?'

'I'm handing myself over to you,' Runo said with a cheerful grin. 'To arrest me. That's your job, isn't it – arresting people?'

'You...' A blink. 'You – are – handing yourself...'

'How much clearer do I have to be? Do you want me to cuff myself too?'

The guard stared at him. 'But...'

Runo got up, groaning. 'Good gods, if I have to do everything here – I suppose the queen wants to be aware you have heroically captured me? Where is she around this time? Study? We might as well go see her to tell her about your triumphant feat and—'

'Have you gone *mad*?' the guard blurted out, staggering after him into the corridor.

'Always been.' He didn't manage to suppress his laughter. The world suddenly looked infinitely brighter – far more than it should, minutes after hearing that his dead body was worth half a crown now. 'But thanks for your concern. Get your sword – excellent – after you, then. Let's go find that queen of yours.'

CHAPTER 12

'Your Majesty?'

Tamar looked up from her letters. Lasha had appeared in the doorway, carrying a stack of books that must weigh twice as much as her own angular body. Almanacs of the wars in the south. Amiran had arranged for them to be sent here, after all.

'Oh, thank you. Put them on the shelf over there, please.'

Her secretary staggered into her room with shuffling steps, looking like she might topple over under the weight of her burden any moment. Tamar hesitated for the shortest moment, then put her pen down and said, 'Do you need a hand?'

Lasha threw her a shocked look. 'What? Oh, no, Your Majesty, it's all under control.'

Even her bony elbows were shaking in her efforts to keep the stack up. Tamar opened her mouth, paused, then shoved back her chair and stood up. Lasha nearly dropped the books.

'Please, Your Majesty – I didn't intend to disturb you!'

So busy making people fear and respect you. She swallowed an unexpected wave of nausea. Five years of working together on a daily basis. Ten years of service in her administration. And still the other woman seemed to believe she might be sent to the gallows for accepting two minutes of help?

'You're not disturbing me at all – my letters can wait a moment.' She forced a smile. 'Here, let me take these...'

It took barely a minute to get the seven books on the shelf where she wanted them. But no matter how often she repeated it was no problem at all, her secretary wouldn't stop apologising as she made her way out of the study again – and the memory of that frightful acquiescence kept Tamar from her letters far longer than the short interruption itself.

'Your Majesty?'

Gocha, this time, standing in her doorway with his hand around his sword and his eyes focussed on some point on the floor between them as usual. Again that twinge of nausea writhed through her guts. She had hired the boy after he arrived at the Red Castle shivering and starving, given him a job and an education with the knights' children of her court, and still he didn't even dare to look her in the eyes?

Making people fear and respect you...

'What is it?'

'Your Majesty – they – they found him.'

At once every trace of lingering nausea vanished. She jolted up with too much vigour and threw her pen down once again – found him. *Finally.* 'Thank the gods – where?'

'In your family's tower, Your Majesty.'

He hadn't moved so much at all, then – why in the world hadn't he? Tamar drew in a shivering breath and said, 'Any other particulars?'

'He – he asks to speak with you again, Your Majesty.' The boy's hand was trembling now, no matter how tightly he clutched it around his sword. 'Your Majesty – forgive me for the impertinence – but will you please not stay alone with him again? They found him with a rope just above your bedroom. He must still be planning to kill you – at least let me stay with you if you *must* have a word with him. Please. I...'

His stammering died away. Still he didn't lift his gaze off the floor. What was he afraid of, that she would laugh at him if their eyes met? Yesterday she'd been frustrated with his protest, she recalled with a sting of regret. Now she felt relieved more than anything else. He might be frightened of her – and that was bad enough in itself – but below the fear, at least he didn't seem to hate her?

'Thank you, Gocha,' she said, standing up. 'I appreciate the sentiment. Nonetheless...'

She hesitated for a moment. What did she think – that she was safe? She had no idea what the assassin was planning to do this time. He might be trying to get to her in some roundabout way – and yet the fear wouldn't come through.

'Your Majesty?'

'I think I'll be fine, Gocha. Could you ask to send him in?'

A shadow slid over his young face, and she knew he had to bite his tongue to stay silent. But he nodded, managed a muffled 'Yes, Your Majesty,' and disappeared again.

Terenti himself brought him in, accompanied by a stocky guard who looked bewildered rather than triumphant. Between the two of them, Runo came sauntering into her room with the most unconcerned smile on his unshaven face, his movements all ease and carelessness. Yesterday it had still been infuriating. But last night she'd seen his eyes, heard the hesitation in his voice. How much of this reckless nonchalance was real, and how much of it was only there to keep that frightened seven-year-old away?

'We found him,' Terenti grumbled before she could speak, pushing Runo half a step forward as if she would have missed him so far. 'Misho here arrested him. Seemed to be making plans to climb into your room over your balcony.'

Runo winked at her, looking even more amused, and Tamar nearly burst out laughing. Oh, gods. Why did he have to be so alarmingly handsome – why did even his *winks* look like shameful proposals? Nonsense, of course. She had to keep her mind clear. He might not be so merciful this time – and yet, that gleam in his eyes...

Our secret, it told her. One of the many we share by now. Us against them – isn't it delightful?

'Ah,' she said. 'Quite disconcerting.'

A dangerous grin broke through on his face. Next to him, Terenti snorted.

'If you want me to make an end to this?'

'Not particularly.' She turned back to Runo, hesitated for a moment too long. *Taavi*, she should say, but how could she get that over her lips? 'You – anything to say?'

'Of course I have something to say, Your Majesty,' he said dryly. 'You know me. I heard something about my life being worth half a kingdom by now?'

'Ah, you picked that up?'

'My heroic captor was so kind to warn me, yes.'

Tamar glanced at Misho, who still looked like a bird had flown against his temple at full speed. The skin around his left eye was turning a faint purple. Runo, on the other hand, seemed oddly unharmed.

Vague suspicions took shape in her mind. 'And you wanted a word with me?'

The smile quirking around his lips confirmed her theory. 'You know how much I appreciate my words with you, Your Majesty.'

'Tamar,' Terenti snapped. 'If you want me to remove this madman...'

'Don't bother. Is he armed?'

'I'm not,' Runo helpfully said before Terenti could answer. 'That invincible warrior taking me prisoner took my knife. Spectacular fight, you should have been there. But if you want to know, I wasn't planning to kill you anyway.'

'I've heard you say that before.'

'And you're still alive, aren't you?'

Not because you didn't try, she wanted to say – but Terenti was still standing mere feet away, and at the sparkle in Runo's eyes, not even the knife he'd pressed to her throat last night seemed more than a silly joke.

'Well,' she said, turning to walk back to her desk. 'If you could be so kind to put a few people at the door, Terenti? If anything happens to me, feel free to treat him however you like.'

'For hell's sake...'

She raised a hand to silence him. Like every army leader worth his salt, her brother-in-law recognised a lost fight when he saw one.

'Don't make me explain this to Amiran,' he snapped, then shoved Misho out of the door and slammed it behind him. As soon the lock clicked shut, Runo burst out laughing, and it was indeed not a laugh that sounded like he would soon strangle her to death.

'Morning to you too, Tamar.'

'Oh, go to hell,' she said, but a warm tingle ran through her as she sank down in her desk chair again. It was not an unpleasant tingle. It was alarmingly pleasant, in fact. 'Had a good night, I understand?'

'Excellent, thanks,' he said cheerfully. 'Nobody shot anything at me for a change.'

Straight to the subject of the conversation. Nothing about the scandalous madness of yesterday. Nothing about – whatever happened last night. Just his own life on the line – had she expected anything else?

But she couldn't deny the quick sliver of disappointment that rose in her.

'No,' she said slowly. 'He turned to more thorough strategies by now, it seems.'

'I'm quite flattered, to tell you the truth.' Runo grinned. 'Nobody has ever considered me worth fifty pieces of gold. But it did get me thinking.'

She raised her eyebrows. 'Oh, you weren't thinking so far? That would explain a little.'

'Doing a stellar job at looking like iron again,' he said. 'And why are you sitting like that?'

'Sitting like what?'

At once his entire posture changed, shoulders back and chest forward, chin up like a huffy lady abandoned by a suitor. He held his position for two heartbeats, then fell down in a chair and grinned his most enchanting grin at her.

'I'm well aware you have a spine. No need to prove it to me.'

Tamar uneasily loosened her shoulders and leaned back in her seat. Her neck breathed a sigh of relief. She felt nearly naked this way, or at least nowhere near queenlike – but then again, he refused to be impressed anyway. She might as well stop trying to be impressive.

'Better?' she said, cursing the flutter of nervousness in her stomach.

'Much better. You nearly look human again.'

'Why, thank you. You're being too generous.'

'I'll stop trying to flatter you, then,' he said dryly. 'Let's have a word about those fifty pieces of gold instead.'

Tamar closed her eyes for a moment. The gold, indeed. 'Are you *very* sure you know nothing of interest?'

'Ah, you had the same thought.' He scratched the back of his head with a nonchalance that made her want to hit him. 'I honestly *thought* I knew nothing of interest. But nobody is paying this kind of money to kill a man who doesn't know anything, wouldn't you say?'

'Yes. So...'

'So I wanted to make you another proposal.'

Her body reacted far too eagerly to that word alone –
as if he'd step around her desk the next moment, tear
her dress off her, and take her again. For hell's sake,
she knew better. And yet – why did he have to look so
insufferably tempting, sitting here handsome and witty
and sharp-minded in her silent working room?

'A – proposal.'

A disconcerting twinkle lit up in his eyes. 'Not one of
those, Tamar. What do you think of me?'

'Oh, pardon me for doubting your honourable
intentions, assassin.' She grimaced. Her body didn't
cool down in the slightest. 'Tell me, then.'

'It's very simple, really. Apparently I know something
about the bastard. You want him dead. I want him dead.
So how about we stop trying to kill each other until
we've figured out what exactly I know and eliminated
his treacherous arse?'

Tamar raised an eyebrow. 'Do I have to remind you
that I'm not—'

'Not killing anyone, I know, I know.' He made a
disparaging gesture. 'Just as a way of speaking.'

'Pretty suggestive way of speaking. Are you trying to
convince yourself you have good reasons to want me
dead?'

He stared at her for a moment too long, and in that
fraction of an instant there was nothing nonchalant to
his expression, nothing amused, nothing playful – just
blank void, something so bland it nearly looked like –

Doubt?

Or was she deluding herself now?

But he recovered within a heartbeat, and nothing looked doubtful about his smile. 'Let's postpone that discussion until we've found your traitor, shall we?'

'As you wish.' Her heart was hammering. Of course she was deluding herself – but then again, could it really mean *nothing* to him? Could he sit here at her desk and not remember the insanity of yesterday? Could he have watched her cry, told her about his past, kissed her goodnight and *not*...

'Wonderful,' he said, interrupting her thoughts. 'We have a deal, then?'

Tamar pressed her lips, fighting the answer for a last moment. Good gods. Closing deals with a Taavi assassin – what was she getting herself into? But he was right, she needed whatever it was that he knew. And then there was the smile he gave her, so bright, so tempting that it was almost encouraging... How could she refuse any deal if he looked at her like that?

You're in trouble, she told herself. If you go on like this, you'll end up slitting your own throat just to please him. But what alternatives did she have? Rejecting his help if it may well save her life?

She looked away. 'We have a deal.'

'Glad to hear,' he said brightly. 'In that case – anyone you killed of late?'

Her breath caught in her throat. 'What?'

Runo jumped up and began ambling through her room again. Even his movements were too easy, too self-assured, a careless elegance to all his strength. Did he know what effect the sight of that muscular body had on her? Did he have any idea of the warmth spiralling through her, her tingling skin remembering the hold of his hands? If he did, his voice betrayed nothing of it – but gods, could he really believe he left her indifferent after all that had occurred in the past twenty-four hours?

'I asked that masked fellow why he wanted you dead,' he said, talking to her bookshelves once again. 'He said you were a murderer. Which seemed self-evident to me at the time, but since you convinced me you're not habitually devouring your subjects' hearts for breakfast...'

'Because I'm a *murderer*?'

He glanced over his shoulder. 'Don't look that shocked, Tamar. He didn't say you slaughtered a score of virgins and bathed in their blood. May have been something pretty innocent.'

She managed a laugh. 'Only you could call murders innocent.'

'I'm quite sure I've seen worse than anything you ever did.' Was it her imagination, or did his smile come out a little dim at those words? 'So – anyone you killed lately?'

Tamar opened her mouth, then hesitated. A murderer. Good gods. Yes, some people were sentenced to death at her court in the past years – but all those convicts were tried by her judges, not by her, and in any case their next of kin shouldn't have fifty pieces of gold lying about. Apart from them –

Anzor.

A cold hand clenched around her heart. That was impossible, wasn't it? Nobody knew about Anzor – nobody but Viviette and Jaghar, and they were the last people on earth who'd ever work with the Taavi Empress. No, it *couldn't* have been because of Anzor. And yet... what if...

'Might it have been Terenti?' she blurted out.

'Terenti? The square fellow who escorted me in so kindly?'

Tamar nodded. Suddenly she barely dared to look him in the eyes.

'Did you kill anyone close to him?'

'Not that I know,' she lied. 'But – well, I'm refusing to set one of his old friends free. If he cares enough about Rusuvan's neck...'

'Oh, Rusuvan,' Runo said cheerfully. 'Caught a glimpse of that one. What did he do?'

'He was the guardian of one of my duchesses when she was a child. Sent her off to Copper Coast just before she got control over her duchy, prevented her from returning, made people address him as the duke – and then when she finally managed to come home, a fortune was missing from the books.' She scoffed. 'He still had the money to buy himself a pretty mansion in Andrough.'

'Ah.' Runo sniggered. 'Doesn't sound like a fellow worth killing a queen for. I'm pretty sure my helper wasn't Terenti, unless he was wearing butcher's heels of ten inches – my man was taller.'

Tamar closed her eyes. Her heart slowly calmed to its usual rhythm. Not her brother-in-law after all, then. Not Pridon or any of her other one-time lovers, either, because she may have hurt their pride, but she certainly didn't *murder* them.

But then it had to be someone else.

Good gods – then it was someone else entirely. Someone she hadn't even *thought* to suspect, someone still walking through the Red Castle. Her breath caught. It could be any nobleman staying here, then. An old grudge, offence taken at one of her decisions. Who knew what people called her a murderer for?

'Is there anything else you know?'

'His hostel room.'

Her eyes flew open. Runo stood before her desk again, arms folded, eyes twinkling at her.

'I beg your pardon?'

'I know his hostel room,' he repeated, a smile breaking through. Gods be damned – why did her knees have to go weak at that smile? He was a murderer. She was being ridiculous. But that rich, tantalising voice... Could anyone sound that seductive by accident?

'Are you very sure?'

'Yes. I could go take a look, if you'd like me to.'

'What – *you*?'

He raised his eyebrows. 'What – anyone else?'

Tamar sagged back in her chair, her mind racing. Anyone else? He was right – she had no idea who she could trust. He at least was the only person who had just as much to win by solving the case, the only person who'd have no reason to lie to her or use his findings as political leverage until her traitor was found. Then again...

'Half the town is out for your head by now.'

'You're the bloody Iron Queen of Redwood,' he said. 'Don't tell me you're afraid of half the town.'

A senseless laugh escaped her. Somehow *everything* seemed easy from his lips. 'Well, fine, I could send some guards along with you – but we'll need quite a few to keep you—'

'No need to do this the forceful way,' he interrupted, shaking his head. 'Give me three guards or so, instruct them to act a little pleasantly towards me. Nobody will consider the possibility I'm that Taavi assassin if I'm chatting around with some men in your armour.' He turned towards her, a devilish twinkle in her eyes. 'Or if you really want to discourage rumours about my identity, you could send one of your noblemen to accompany me.'

'If I must risk my noblemen's life for your little walk in town, you can be sure you're getting one I wouldn't miss too much,' Tamar said sourly. 'Are you sure that's the kind of company you're looking for?'

'The worse, the better. At least it will give me something to laugh about along the way.'

His reckless grin was convincing, admittedly. The grin of a man with not a care in the world. But that wasn't what he was, and with that knowledge in mind...

'Yes,' she said slowly. 'And as long as you can laugh about the world, you don't have to think about it, isn't it?'

Again he froze for a moment, his laugh faltering. 'Must you?'

'You're significantly less infuriating when you stop smirking at everything,' Tamar said, and the corners of his lips tugged up again.

'Pity. I quite like you infuriated.'

She raised an eyebrow, her heart skipping a beat. 'Are you stupid or suicidal?'

'Just easily bored,' he said. 'So. Can I go take a look at that bloody hostel? Quite eager to find the bastard by now, honestly.'

Tamar pulled a sheet of parchment from her drawer without an answer, dipped her pen in the ink, and scribbled down the usual quick note, cursing her trembling fingers – *allow the bearer of this message all required assistance, he works in my name.* Runo's footsteps made their way around the desk as she wrote until he stood just behind her, close enough to read along. His presence against her back was like the warmth of the sun, a temptation that made her forget for a fraction of a heartbeat what she was doing, or why.

'Working in your name.' He seemed to be tasting the words. 'Honoured.'

'Flattering me, hm?'

He laughed. 'Which is not the same as lying.'

'You're still impossible,' Tamar said. The strange warmth surging through her didn't allow any more intelligent answers. Runo laughed again, a laugh that carried memories of his lips on hers, his hands taking possession of her – and yet he didn't touch her.

A Taavi assassin. She couldn't possibly *want* him to touch her.

With a brusque movement she reached for the top drawer of her desk, plucked her signet ring out, and closed it. Not quick enough.

'Two rings?' He leaned over her shoulder to re-open the drawer and pluck out the second one. Between his quick fingers, the boar seal didn't look nearly as threatening as usual.

'My late husband's,' Tamar said curtly, picking up the nearest candle. The fire felt dangerous in her hands at the mention of the word. She didn't want to think about Anzor now – not with that murder accusation still ringing in her ears, not with Runo standing mere inches away from her.

'Did you love him?' he said.

She nearly burnt her fingers. 'What?'

'Your husband.' He was still turning the ring between his fingers as if to estimate its worth. Tamar clenched her teeth and grabbed her wax, holding the bar into the small flame until a few drops dripped onto the parchment. Blood red. Not a thought she should have allowed into her mind now.

'None of your concern,' she said, but it didn't sound as convincing as she'd hoped. Behind her, Runo chuckled.

'An answer for an answer, Tamar.'

'Did I get any particular answers from you lately?'

'I told you about your traitor?'

'To save your own skin as much as mine. Doesn't count.'

'Well, fine.' He threw the ring back in its place and sauntered around her desk again, turning to look at her. Even ten feet away he was still far, far too close. 'Ask me anything in return, then. Did you love him?'

She was grasping for straws now. 'Why would you want to know?'

'Because you haven't answered me yet. Usually means you're hiding something of interest. So I assume the answer is negative.'

Tamar looked up from the melting wax. His voice sounded light, nearly cheerful even, but for a moment, there was nothing amused to his eyes.

Would he laugh? Would he act like her torment of a marriage was a joke like all else in the world?

For a single senseless moment, it seemed the most important question in the world.

'He was a terrible person,' she said slowly, and the words came out like a challenge, a test. 'I spent twelve years hating him from the depths of my heart and didn't shed a genuine tear when he died. Does that answer your question?'

He didn't laugh. He didn't even joke.

'It does.'

Tamar averted her eyes, back to the puddle of wax before her. As she pressed her ring into it, Runo resumed his rounds through her room – calm, collected footsteps, sounding nearly expectant. Only when she pulled her ring from the wax did he stand still. When she looked up, he was observing her with strangely earnest eyes – that damned deceptive look. As if he cared. As if he still wanted her to believe he cared.

'No questions back?' he said.

Tamar opened her mouth. Then closed it again. She had questions, yes, a hundred of them – what are you *doing*? What are you trying to make me do? What do you want from me, what does it mean to you, do you feel even half the confusion that you stir in me whenever you're around? But that tangled clew of thoughts only shaped four simple words on her lips, echoing his own –

'Did you like it?' she blurted out.

For a heartbeat he froze. Then his gaze swerved to her desk, to the spot where he had kissed her yesterday, and back to her face.

'Tamar...'

Their eyes met, and he didn't finish his sentence. No amusement in his look, not a trace of mockery – just a nearly painful gleam, like a plea to take back her question. Again something stirred in her, and this time it wasn't confusion alone.

'I was trying to survive,' he said slowly.

She managed a smile. 'As a wise man once told me, that doesn't need to mean you didn't find it enjoyable.'

For a moment he stood paralysed; then abruptly he moved forward, five long strides towards her, and grabbed her off her chair before she could shrink back. With a single turn he pressed her against the wall, his scorching body locking her against the plaster. An incredulous grin grew on his face. '*What* did you call me, Tamar?'

She wanted to answer, but didn't manage – without warning her laughter returned, shaking through her and blocking all sensible speech. Runo's grin broadened in reply. Lowering his head to hold her gaze, he repeated, 'What did you call me?'

'You'll answer me first.' It took all she had not to burst out in hysterical giggles at the sight of the playful twinkle in his eyes. 'I'm not giving you any answers before you tell me...'

'If I liked it?'

'If...'

If it meant anything to you, she wanted to say – but she realised the impossibility of that sentence just in time, and her voice died away without a conclusion. With a shock she became aware of herself again, of this silent room, this situation – the fact that she stood here flirting with a Taavi assassin. The sanity returned to his face at the same moment. The amusement sank from his eyes; his grin came down. He moved back half an inch, away from the wall, away from her. He looked down, avoiding her gaze.

For a moment their heavy breath was all she heard, the rhythm of it mingling in the mere inches of void between them.

'Runo...' she whispered.

'You're not making this easier for either of us.' His voice was so hoarse it was barely audible. 'Is this really a question you must ask?'

He didn't meet her eyes. His breath still came too quickly – and yet he didn't let go of her.

'If I were still doubting, you now convinced me', Tamar said.

'Because I won't answer you?'

'Usually means you're hiding something of interest, isn't it?'

'Oh, damn you.' A joyless chuckle. 'Why are you doing this now, then? Trying to save your life again?'

She wrestled her arm from his grip and grabbed his chin, the stubble of his unshaven cheeks rough against her fingers. Runo froze at the touch, but moved along when she tugged up his head to meet his eyes. A haunted look, nearly bewildered. Again her body stirred.

'You kissed me,' she said.

'Shouldn't have.'

'And yet you did.'

His lips twitched, but he didn't answer.

'You didn't kill me. You're still not killing me. You come falling in asking about my bloody *husband* – so yes, this really is a question I must ask. Did you like—'

'I didn't.'

It came out too loud, too fast. Tamar slowly loosened her fingers from his chin, a nauseous disappointment welling up in her.

'You—'

'That is to say,' he continued, sharply, 'it would be a disgraceful understatement to say I *liked* it. Is that what you want to hear? I want you, fine. I damn well dreamt of you, if you really want to know – and then what? I'm still supposed to kill you. If I ever want to see my home again, you *will* have to die – so can you please just accept that fucking you sore and spent is not exactly the first of my priorities now?'

His voice died away in a panting silence. A silence in which she should push him away and run before he could act on his words and strangle her to death after all. And yet...

His arousal stirred against her lower belly. His hands tensed on her hips. A feeling like threat, but had any threat ever felt so good?

'I thought to have understood you have no intention of killing me now, though,' she said.

'Tamar—'

She leaned over before he could finish that sentence, planted her lips on his to smother the rest of his words, and he kissed her back as if it were the last thing he'd ever do in life.

CHAPTER 13

What in the world was he *doing*?

The rules of the game were simple, so ridiculously simple. Don't get attached. Don't desire, don't need. But Tamar kissed him with desperate, ravenous lips, and the rest of the world lost its colour at the taste of her – satin, salt, seduction, a sensation of the softest, deepest rosewood pink. In a reflex Runo wrapped his fingers around her wrists and opened his mouth to her, tongues twisting in a fierce battle for control. Her fists clenched under his hands. He felt her pulse racing just below her skin, the rhythm mingling with the rush of his heartbeat in his own ears. Her stifled moans, half triumph and half pleasure, completed the harmony. The desire tore through him like a senseless wildfire, blurring every rule Raulinna had ever instilled in him. He wanted her, with such intensity it felt nearly like hate; the need to possess her pulsed through every inch of his body as he kissed her, pinning her against the wall and savouring her eagerness, her lips begging for his affection. Nothing in the world could ever compare to this, a powerful woman trusting him enough to be powerless in his arms...

Trusting him.

With a gasp he drew back, breaking the wet, wicked wildness of their kiss. Tamar let her head fall back against the wall with a breathless groan. Glistening lips, smouldering eyes, every glorious inch of her daring him to throw her over that desk again, pull up her skirts and make her feel exactly what he had wanted to do to her last night.

But hell's sake, not if she trusted him. Not if she expected him, genuinely expected him, to spare her life in return for her willingness.

'Bad idea.' His voice was a growl. She was too close, her body too tempting against the hard, hungry need of his erection. 'Terrible idea. Don't expect this to make me any more pliable or—'

She interrupted him with a husky laugh. 'What made you think I want you any more pliable?'

"*Listen*,' he hissed, pinning her wrists against the wall. Gods be damned. *Want you*. He was so hard it hurt now, every vein in his body pulsing with savage lust at the promise of her body. 'This is not going to save your life. Do you hear me? This doesn't mean—'

'Might as well enjoy myself for once, then,' she retorted, lip curling up. 'That was your lesson, wasn't it? Coming back from it now?'

'Oh, you're trying to teach *me* a lesson now?'

She tried to move forward to kiss him, but he didn't give way, pressing her wrestling body back against the wall as she gasped in frustration. A laugh escaped him.

'And you're still not the one in charge here, Tamar.'

She sagged back against the wall and closed her eyes. Heaving breasts, clenched jaws – but her wrists relaxed under his grip. Oh, for hell's sake. An irresistible surrender. Not a victory he could claim, not if his loyalty and good sense meant a damn to him – but then there was the tense expectation on her face. The power and grandness of her, his to take.

Did she want him? Did she *truly* want him?

'Kneel,' he said.

Her eyes flew open. A breathless, incredulous silence, lips parted to protest – but no objection came out. Runo held her gaze as he slowly released her arms and took half a step back, separating their bodies, driving cold air between them. She didn't move. A filthy triumph roared through him.

'Kneel, Tamar.'

'You...' A baffled laugh, and yet she didn't break their mutual gaze. 'You *bastard*.'

'Not the most pleasant thing to say.' The high of his nearing victory was making him light-headed, an addictive, reckless sensation of power. 'Seemed to me that you were looking for something. But if you're not, I suppose I'll leave and—'

'Don't go.'

She blurted out the words too fast, then clenched her jaws as if to take them back – but no amount of regret could make him forget how desperate that plea had fallen from her lips. His grin grew on his face all by itself, fuelled by the hunger roaring in him as much as by the hunger in her eyes.

'Your pick, Tamar.'

For another moment she hesitated, eyes searching his face for traces of jest, lips moving without a sound. Then, with stiff, uneasy movements, she came away from the wall and sank through her knees before him, breath faltering as she hit the floor.

'Happy now, assassin?'

He chuckled. 'Pretty sure you could make me happier, if you feel so inclined.'

Her glance up at him was a knife stab, and yet she didn't move away from him, and held his gaze. Burning brown eyes, pupils dilated with desire. Her stare was testing him, warning him perhaps – but the aching desire flushing through him paid no heed to tests and warnings.

'Well?' he said, answering her glare with his most innocent expression. 'I thought you wanted me, Your Majesty?'

With a muttered curse, she lifted her hands to the buttons of his trousers and began to loosen them with quick, impatient yanks. She closed her eyes the moment his erection broke free from the sturdy linen, but even that couldn't hide the tension on her face, the lust, the anticipation, the shame, the dazzled elation. Her fingers closed around the base of his shaft, and the pressure of her touch alone was enough to drive a groan from his lips. As in a dream he watched her lean over, slowly and deliberately. The queen of Redwood. Defeated, suddenly. Kneeling before him on the floor of her own study, her slender hand around his scorching flesh, her lips parting to take him in...

Then her tongue found his tip, and there was nothing dreamlike about the world anymore, about the bolt of pleasure that seared through him. He grabbed for the wall to keep standing without taking his gaze off her. At his feet, Tamar barely seemed aware of his watching eyes as she ran her tongue along his length, tasting him like candy, sucking on him with warm, hungry lips until every inch of him ached for release. She looked nearly drunk on his taste, eager and exalted, shivers running through her at every muffled curse she pulled from him.

'Tamar...' he groaned.

She didn't look up, but took him into her mouth even deeper in reply, tongue twisting around his cock. Runo clenched his free hand into her hair and managed a grunted laugh.

'Enjoying yourself, Your Majesty?'

'Don't know why I would,' she murmured, the words barely distinguishable. 'A man like you?'

A sting of arousal ran through him like poison. 'Pull up your skirt.'

She slowly let go of him, glancing up with glazed eyes. At his smile, she averted her face and hitched up her skirt with shaking hands. Runo crouched and slipped a hand underneath the black silk, brushing past the rosy skin of her inner thighs, the red bush of curls... Then he found the swollen lips behind, and the tight warmth clenching around him as he pressed a fingertip into her. Her breath caught, but she didn't move.

She was undeniably drenched.

He couldn't suppress his smile. Inches away from him, something twitched around Tamar's lips – but she didn't avert her gaze.

'Gave yourself away, I'm afraid,' he said softly. 'Turn around. On your knees.'

She turned her back towards him and bent over at his first nudge, supporting herself with both hands on the wooden floor. Runo pulled her skirts aside and trailed a finger along her glistening flesh again, savouring the sight of her, pink and pooling up in anticipation. She gasped as he passed that most sensitive spot between her lips. 'Runo...'

He laughed and pressed two fingers into her at once, stretching her open. 'You don't have the faintest idea how good my name sounds on your hungry lips.'

A moan escaped her. 'Runo – please...'

'Say that again?'

'Oh, damn you – *please*.' Her voice was giving in. 'I just want – I want...'

He positioned himself behind her, guiding his tip to her entrance. 'You want?'

A breathless silence, just a heartbeat. Then she whispered, 'You.'

He could no longer hold back, then, could no longer control himself. With a single thrust he buried himself into her wetness, the world blurring around him, his thoughts evaporating. He was nothing but his aching need for her, nothing but the hands on her hips and the scorching steel slamming into her. She moaned along with every thrust, faster and faster, her voice rising as the tension in his loins built to unbearable heights. Far too quickly he gave in, powerless against the pleasure tearing through him. His climax found him in merciless waves of ecstasy, pulsing through him for what seemed an eternity, until he was left empty and spent inside her with the world still hazy around him and her luscious body all his eyes could grasp.

He drew out of her without releasing her hips, pulled her back against him, wrapped his arms around her. They rolled over onto the wooden floor together, her shivering body pressed against his chest, his face buried in her red locks, the world a mess of silk and linen, hands and lips, sticky wetness and glowing skin. Under his fingers he found the slick warmth between her thighs, then the spot that made her gasp in breathless pleasure. She pressed tighter against him as he rubbed that sensitive bud with quick, circling strokes, savouring the sensation of her drenched flesh, her body arching into his caresses. With her eyes closed, her lips parted, her stifled moans rising higher and higher, she looked so strangely innocent in his arms, so blissfully unburdened. Hell, he wanted to keep her like this. He wanted to spend the next three hours watching her elated face, wanted to hear that quiet delight in her moans until the sun set again... But her orgasm ripped through her within moments, clenching her against him with a nearly helpless cry, and he was left with a strange mixture of satisfaction and unfulfilled desire itching on his fingertips, a nearly painful awareness of all he still wanted to feel, see, taste. So much more to discover – so, so much more to discover...

'Runo,' she whispered again, her voice hoarse, and this time there was no plea or question to his name. He leaned over and kissed the hot skin below her ear, then her cheek, her temple. In his arms she felt like everything he ever held dear in his life.

'Tamar,' he whispered back.

A blissful smile slid over her face as she nestled herself against his chest even tighter. Runo lowered his head onto the wooden floor and closed his eyes. The last high of his orgasm finally faded away, and in its place a rosy feeling grew in him – a feeling dangerously close to the comfort of her blankets last night, the warmth of her fire and the brilliance of her smiles. No feeling he could allow anywhere close, but how in the world would he push it aside again?

'Could think of worse ways to spend my last days,' she muttered, and despite himself he chuckled.

'There are no last days until we've found that traitor of yours.'

She sighed. 'You could just – not make haste finding him.'

'Perhaps.' He came up on his elbow again. 'At the very least I suppose I could take a break for the night, if I can find myself a place to sleep.'

Tamar turned to meet his gaze, the gleam in her eyes both sceptical and strangely hopeful. For a moment she only looked at him in hesitant silence; then, resting her forehead against his shoulder, she whispered, 'I might have a key for you.'

He laid his hand around the back of her head and held her, immersing himself in her fragrance of sweet rosewood and salty lust until his thoughts stopped reeling and his heart found its usual rhythm again.

It burnt in his pocket when he walked out of the Red Castle an hour later – that rusty little key his masked co-conspirator had given him to kill Tamar mere days ago. Now given to him again, by her this time, to kill the same masked bastard, and also to find his way to her bed tonight. Little of it made sense, and yet his heart jolted a little every time he brushed his fingertips over the shape of the metal in his pocket.

He felt like another man entirely as he walked down that path to town again, in clean clothes, shaven, and accompanied by a cocky duke and a handful of guards who made not the slightest attempt to separate his head from his body. Even his mind barely seemed his own anymore. Tamar still occupied three quarters of his thoughts, the memory of her lips burning in his loins, her voice whispering that single word at him – *You...* Gone was the simple mission that had kept him occupied last time he walked this road between town and castle; gone were the urgency of his instructions, the fear of failure. The gap between himself and his memories was so substantial that he barely felt addressed when the man beside him cleared his throat halfway to town and started, 'So – you're working for the Empress?'

The title came out with all the usual scorn in this part of the world. Runo shrugged, too deep in thought to make the effort of taking offence.

'Deducted that correctly, brother. Do you have any issues with her?'

The duke snorted. 'Well, issues...'

They walked on in silence for some minutes. Then the other man again cleared his throat and declared, 'In my opinion, it can't be natural, a woman ruling an entire empire on her own.'

Runo nearly stopped mid-step. *Natural?* Why don't you come back to Raulinna with me, he almost said, let's see how natural her power appears to you by the time you're playing kickball with your own head. But another part of his mind intervened, the part that still hadn't fully left Tamar's study.

'There's a queen sitting on your own throne,' he said, raising his eyebrows. 'How is that any less unnatural?'

'It isn't.'

Runo raised his eyebrows even higher, unsure if he should laugh or punch the idiot in the face. All of a sudden he understood the tired amusement in Tamar's voice – *I'll just send Pridon with you. Don't bother too much to bring him back...*

'It isn't?' he repeated. If for no other reason, at least they could have a good laugh about this tonight. Next to him, the duke snorted.

'Men are rulers. Women are nurturers. That's the natural order of things.'

'Ah,' Runo said. 'Your queen didn't make a terribly nurturing impression on me so far.'

'Because she doesn't have a husband,' Pridon immediately retorted, sounding far too pleased with himself. 'Just like that Empress of yours. You see? Forces them to act like men. By the time the queen remarries, she'll see...'

He didn't finish his sentence, but his next snort spoke volumes. Runo glanced aside. The man walked unpleasantly straight all of a sudden, oddly resembling a weasel showing off his new clothes. Something ugly twisted in his guts, a feeling that reminded him a little too urgently of the knife in his pocket.

'Ambitions?' he said, and Pridon scoffed.

'Stay out of the matters of nobility, you dog.'

'Oh, just call me Runo,' he said cheerfully. 'No need for all that formality.'

The duke opened his mouth, then blinked, frowned, and shut his mouth again. Runo chuckled. Neither of them continued the conversation, and they walked on in mutually disgusted silence the rest of the way – past the villas closest to the castle, the expensive restaurants, the goldsmiths and jewellers; then past the respectable workmen's houses; and finally through the narrow streets where the poorest had their lodgings above the taverns and the gambling dens. Tamar's guards didn't flinch, but Pridon's nose wrinkled deeper with every step into the underbelly of the city.

'Are you sure...'

'Just around the corner,' Runo said.

He expected the quiet, shadowy street in which he'd arrived a few nights ago – no passers-by except a few poor souls, at least until sunset. But when they rounded the corner, a decent crowd had gathered between the narrow houses, buzzing like only a crowd at a site of tragedy could.

Centred, he realised a moment later, around the little hostel where he met his masked helper on that fateful night.

'Good gods,' Pridon muttered behind him. 'What is going on?'

The first people caught sight of them then. The crowd went eerily silent within a heartbeat, parting to let them through – a straight line to the front door, where a grubby city guard stood leaning against the post. The man jolted up immediately.

'My lords!'

'He's not...' Pridon began.

Runo didn't have the patience to wait for his correction. Nodding at the crowd behind him, he stepped before the duke and said, 'What in the world is happening here, brother?'

'What – that's not what you're here for?' The guard grimaced. 'Innkeeper was found with his throat slit this morning.'

Behind him Pridon cried out something sharp and shocked and utterly useless. Runo gave himself a single heartbeat to regain his composure; then he gestured the guard to step aside and slipped into the hall before anyone could object. 'Where?'

'Room behind the counter.'

He found three other men in armour in that room, counting money and scanning documents. In the middle of the room, like a dramatic décor piece, the corpse of the innkeeper still sat at his small desk, an expression of eternal bewilderment on his plump face, a dark cascade of drying blood over his throat and chest. Practiced cut, Runo concluded with one glance. Someone who knew how to handle a weapon. Then again – that would be the case for most noblemen at Tamar's court.

'And you are?' one of the men groused.

He pulled Tamar's sealed letter from his pocket. The sight of her crest alone softened the suspicion on their faces.

'Does he have anything to do with the queen?'

'Perhaps,' Runo said, shrugging. 'Perhaps not. Could I take a look at room twenty-four?'

They exchanged a few quick looks, but concluded quickly he could do little harm; one of them pulled a key from the rack beside the innkeeper's desk and threw it into Runo's hands. Closer to the door he heard Pridon's voice approaching – no time to lose.

'If you can keep that fellow occupied for a few moments,' he said with a nod in the duke's direction, 'I won't complain. Back in a minute.'

The men seemed rather amused at that request – he heard them elaborate on the details of the case with striking enthusiasm as he sprinted up the stairs to the second floor himself. His head was spinning. Too much of a coincidence for the poor sod to have died exactly *this* night – a night in which the masked traitor had been in town to hand out fifty pieces of gold, knowing that Runo was aware of his lodgings here. But if the bastard killed the innkeeper who might know his face, he likely took the time to destroy the rest of the evidence too.

At least nobody else had set foot into the room yet. That might help a little.

The door swung open without noise, revealing a hostel room quite like all others – narrow bed, narrow window, narrow desk, everything as uncomfortable as a piece of furniture could be without becoming utterly useless. Runo stepped inside, shut the door, and made a quick round through the drawers and closets. All empty. As he should have expected – the man would simply have packed all his belongings last night, thrown his documents into the fire, and...

Wait. The fire.

With one step he was at the fireplace. A sizeable heap of ash indeed, suggesting someone burnt half a library in this room last night.

He sank down on his knees, grabbed his knife, and went through the cinders, stirring them slowly and systematically to make sure he wouldn't overlook the smallest piece of parchment. Here and there some scorched shreds emerged from the destruction, but only some of them showed traces of writing, and never more than a few letters. The ash-pan, then – no, still mostly useless shreds – but *there*...

He snatched the fleck of red from the ash before it could get buried again. Half of a wax seal, its contours softened by the fire that had burnt close, but still reasonably preserved. It must have fallen into the tray nearly immediately. Runo could still recognise –

A boar.

His eyes widened. A seal he'd held in his fingers mere hours ago.

For a moment he sat frozen, impressions coming at him from all sides. *My late husband's.* The dead Anzor's seal, in this ash-pan in room twenty-four. *He was a terrible person.* Burn scars on her arms, her body giving in under his fingers. *She's a murderer...*

Behind him the door slammed open, and Pridon's voice burst into the room. 'What in the *world* did you think you were doing, you dog?'

'Nothing much,' Runo said, slipping the seal into his pocket as he got to his feet. 'Sorry for wasting your time. We can return to the castle.'

The duke blinked. 'What?'

'There's nothing to be found here,' he said, stepping out into the corridor without looking back at the empty little room. 'He must have known we'd be here soon. He burnt everything already.'

CHAPTER 14

'So,' Runo's voice broke the silence behind her.

Tamar jolted around, heart slamming into her throat, and hastily shoved her book back on the pile with the rest. Spine to the wall – he didn't need to know about her sudden interest in the history of the Cuvri War. He'd shown up in her doorway without knocking, head cocked aside, hands in his pockets. In his new clothes, his cheeks no longer covered in stubble, he barely even looked like a Taavi assassin anymore – just another man at her court, and a damned handsome one at that.

'You're back already?'

A grin broke through. 'Did you miss me?'

'Spent every minute pining for you,' she said, rolling her eyes to hide the fact it was not a full lie at all. Her tongue seemed unable to let go of the taste of him, her body unwilling to forget her impossible surrender at his feet. 'A miracle that I haven't yet died from unfulfilled longing, like some useless fairy-tale heroine.'

Runo cocked his head aside. 'Want to know something about bad liars, Tamar?'

'What?'

'It's obvious when they're not lying, too,' he said, sinking down in a chair at her desk.

She scoffed. 'You arrogant—'

'Yes, yes, I know. Let's have a word about something a little more urgent.'

She had already opened her mouth to object, but something about the look in his eyes, the way he rested his elbows on his knees as he leaned over with those last words, suggested the matter of her unfulfilled pining was not the most dangerous subject on his mind by far.

'Did you find anything?'

He met her gaze. Pursed his lips. Drew in a deep breath.

He said, 'Did you murder your husband?'

It took her a heartbeat, a full, slow heartbeat, to know she hadn't misheard him. That she hadn't started hallucinating, her guilty conscience hearing the echoes of Anzor's violent death in every sentence spoken around her. That he had asked...

Then she saw the look in his eyes – no amusement, no mockery – and she knew it was barely a question at all.

'What?' she managed.

He stayed silent, eyes following her every move.

'Why – why would you think...'

His hand disappeared into his pocket and re-appeared holding a scrap of scorched parchment, covered by a blot of dark red wax. Even from ten feet away, even if the edges of the seal had melted a little, she recognised the image immediately.

'What?' she whispered again.

'He realised we'd find the hostel,' Runo said slowly, his voice unusually earnest. 'Killed the innkeeper who probably knew his face. Burnt all the parchment he kept in his room, but this little thing managed to escape. Found it in the ash-pan. Looking suspiciously like—'

'Anzor's seal,' she finished quietly.

He looked up. 'Which seems to suggest that someone linked to your husband called you a murderer.'

She opened her mouth, then closed it again. What could she say? No. No, this is nonsense. How dare you accuse me of such a crime? Take it back before I have you hanged – none of that would impress *him*, and either way she didn't want to hang him...

'Tamar,' he said.

Cold sweat trickled along her spine. Without thinking she staggered back, away from him, as if that would take the dangerous edge off his words – no. It was impossible. Nobody knew the truth about Anzor – *nobody* – and *he* should know least of all, with his damned Taavi loyalties and his sharp eyes and his delirious touches –

'Tamar.'

'No,' she whispered without knowing the next word she would speak, 'no, that's not – I wouldn't – why would you...'

She hadn't heard him get up. He appeared out of thin air, close enough to touch her. 'Tamar, calm down. There's no need to—'

'No *need*?'

'What do you think I'll do?' His voice was a beacon of calm, the last log of wood she could grab before drowning. 'Gather your nobles and dramatically accuse you? Call you a monster and a disgrace? I'm a lot of things, but not a hypocrite. Calm down.'

Even that sounded easy from his lips – calm down. Come on, Tamar, you can do it. Just a few deep breaths, slow and steady. Wipe your sweaty hands and swallow the gall in your throat, steel your shoulders and look up again. He's not a threat. He's not...

He's not blaming you?

She didn't know the look in his eyes – something defeated, a sadness that lay deeper than any joking nonchalance, any seductive darkness she had seen on his face. She felt herself shrinking under that look, defences crumbling like walls of sand until she couldn't even remember her own lies.

'I killed him,' she whispered.

'I know,' he said.

'I – I'm sorry – I—'

'Why would you be?'

Tamar stared at him. He smiled a soft, sad smile and held out his arms, beckoning her closer. Without thinking she stepped into his embrace, burying her face in the warmth of his muscular chest – murderer, her thoughts whispered at her, you're a murderer, and someone knows. Somewhere, someone in the Red Castle knows.

'Your arms,' Runo said, interrupting the menacing circles of her own mind. 'Those burn scars. Was that him?'

She nodded. His arms tensed around her.

'Twelve years.'

She nodded again. He rested his lips against the crown of her head and held her, running his fingers through her hair as they stood – a hug so tender, so comforting that she wanted to cry and hide in his arms forever.

'When he was drunk,' she whispered. 'Or angry. Or both. It wasn't always the candles. Usually he just beat me – but when he was particularly vexed...'

'You never sent *him* to the gallows?'

'Needed his armies.' How often had she repeated that sentence to herself? 'Redwood needed the stability.'

'Tamar...'

He didn't continue, but the arms around her didn't give way. Arms feeling like safety. A body like a rock, smelling of summer and spices and something that was just sheer masculinity, a smell dangerously close to the taste of him. Not something to think about now – but he still carried the key to her room in his pocket, and at that thought even the memory of Anzor couldn't get much of a grip on her.

'Tamar?' he said again, softer now.

'Hm?'

'Don't know if it means a damn to you, but I'd like to apologise. For ever believing you were doing any of this for your own pleasure.'

She stiffened, then turned her head to look up at him, at the part of his face she could see while pressed against his shoulder. Something tensed around the corners of his lips, words he only barely kept inside. Apologise. For believing the worst of her. *He* – the man who made such an effort to believe nothing in the world ever meant a thing to him –

And yet he didn't shrug Anzor aside. Yet he didn't shrug *her* aside.

'It does mean a damn to me,' she said.

So you *do* care, she wanted to add. Does all of this mean anything to you after all, then – do *I* mean anything to you? But he let go of her already and fell back down in his chair before she could speak, all vulnerability gone up in smoke at once.

'So, if I may ask...' So pleasantly conversational, like a man discussing the weather. 'How did you do it?'

'How – what?'

'Poison, wasn't it?'

'Belladonna.' She hesitated. 'Why would you...'

'Professional interest,' he said. 'And it may help us figure out who else might know. At least some people may have suspected you'd rather get rid of him.'

'Which wouldn't help them much. General account is that it was an attempt at my life.'

He raised an eyebrow. 'Tell me more.'

'Dropped it into my own glass,' she said, closing her eyes. 'He got drunk and started yelling for more to drink. He always did. I offered him my wine. Then cried and whined when he dropped off his chair and choked. Threw the rest of the poison into the abyss the next day, and—'

'The *abyss*?'

'We were at Rock Hall.'

Runo blew out his cheeks. 'Hell's sake. You thought it would be a good idea to poison the bastard right under the bloody spy king's nose?'

'Not the king yet, at that time.'

'No less dangerous for it, from what I've heard.'

'No – but I didn't want Anzor's soldiers around. And...' She hesitated. 'They – they did find out, admittedly.'

'They?'

'Jaghar and Viviette.'

'Ah,' he said slowly. 'So people *do* know.'

Tamar rubbed her temple. 'I would be highly surprised if Jaghar started enlisting Taavi assassins, though.'

'Admittedly.' He sounded bitter now. 'Bastard killed seven of my colleagues in the past decade alone, if I kept count correctly.'

'I don't remember Rock Hall killing any of them.'

Runo threw her a sharp look. 'Sending them back into the Empress's hands after pulling the Empire's secrets from them pretty much boils down to the same thing, doesn't it?'

'No,' Tamar said. 'No, I actually don't think that boils down to the same thing at all.'

He stared at her for a moment, thoughts visibly turning behind his eyes. Then, with a brusque shrug, he turned away. 'In any case, is there a chance your lovely friend from Rock Hall spread the secret?'

'I don't see why he would. He covered it up in the first place.'

'He did?' He groaned. 'Well. Unexpectedly kind for a man of his reputation.'

It was Viviette first, she nearly said, walking into my room with those clever green eyes and prying a confession out of me – Viviette, too, who had insisted that nobody would ever find out about the truth of the case. But she probably shouldn't tell the Taavi Empress too much about that unnervingly sharp mind on Rock Hall's throne, or about her personal suspicions that something had been going on between the now-spouses long before Viviette was even sent off to marry another man.

'Perhaps you should accept by now that reputations aren't always correct,' she said instead, and he gave her a wry grin.

'Trying to make a point?'

'No points you haven't yet made yourself.'

Again he hesitated for the shortest moment. 'Shouldn't we return to our investigation?'

It felt unnervingly good, seeing him wrestling with himself for those minuscule moments. *Something* was working against the Empress's orders in his mind, something he didn't want to see – something he didn't *dare* to see perhaps. He did care, then. Which shouldn't mean so much to her, not as long as both of their lives were still in danger. But perhaps – later – after the traitor was found...

'Fine,' she said, forcing herself to nod. 'The investigation. Any brilliant ideas as to how people could have figured out how exactly Anzor died?'

'Did you speak about it with people?'

'No.'

'Not even with Jaghar and Viviette?'

'I don't think...'

She froze mid-sentence. A memory hit her, vague but frightening – she didn't *speak* with them about it, no, but their correspondence...

'Ah,' Runo said, sounding far too satisfied again. 'We're getting somewhere.'

With three steps she was at the shelf that carried her letter folders, just below the stack of Cuvrian almanacs. Not the letters from the Riverlands – not those from Androrough – *there*, the sizeable leather folder with her Rock Hall correspondence of the last years. She flicked it open with trembling fingers and browsed through the pile of parchment. Last summer – it must have been somewhere in the summer –

There. *Dear Tamar*, Viviette's handwriting.

'What are you looking for, exactly?' Runo said.

'A letter from Viviette.' Her eyes flew over the lines. 'Made a little joke in one of my letters, a few months after the wedding – something about the fools who wouldn't shut up about Jaghar being Androughan by birth. Anyway, she wrote back...' She cleared her throat, her eyes settling on those treacherous words. *'As to my Androughan savage of a husband – yes, it seems even half of Rock Hall still expects him to drag me around by my hair any day. Quite amusing, frankly. But don't worry, I have no need for pinches of belladonna or any similar measures.'*

She looked up, clenching her lips. Runo nodded slowly.

'Someone might have read that.'

'If someone was mad enough to read my private letters.'

'We're speaking about someone who doesn't mind hiring Taavi assassins to murder his own queen, Tamar,' he said dryly. 'I doubt he'd draw the line at reading letters if he suspected something after Anzor's death.'

'Oh, gods.' She closed her eyes. Only now did the realisation fully come through. Someone could know – someone *knew*. 'Oh, gods – but who would even care?'

'That's what I should be asking you.' His voice was still light and calm, but earnest enough to know he wasn't mocking her. 'Who would want to avenge Anzor? Except for that Terenti fellow we already excluded – any other family members?'

'Their younger brothers haven't been at the Red Castle for a year,' she said hoarsely. 'Terenti is the only one who shows up regularly. A few cousins, but none that were particularly fond of him – a mistress or five, but I've made sure they wouldn't return to the court after his death.'

'Is that supposed to mean you threw them out?'

'It's supposed to mean I'm sending them five pieces of gold every year, with two more for each child, on the condition that they never show their faces around the castle again.' She looked away, fumbling Viviette's letter back into the folder. 'I know what he was like. Can't blame them for – well, him.'

Runo stayed silent. When she eventually looked up, the folder back in its place on the shelf, he was staring at her with earnest, contemplative eyes.

'You're not much of an iron queen at all, are you?'

'Well,' she said, a sour grin breaking through, 'I must admit I didn't ask them very *nicely*. I doubt they got out of our last encounter with many warm feelings about me.'

'But it's unlikely they enlisted a Taavi murderer to kill the person paying them a comfortable salary,' he said, shaking his head. 'Anyone else? More children you don't know about?'

'There are more children. May as well be dozens of them. He had quite a reputation already before we married.'

'Well, that's promising.' He pinched his lips. 'Anyone who might have a list?'

She closed her eyes. 'I know he had a list of sorts – the family secretaries made sure to send the women some regular money, as far as I know. I never bothered to take a look. I suppose Terenti may still have an overview, but I doubt he'll happily give it to me.'

'Brotherly love or brotherly embarrassment?'

'Bit of both.'

Runo sighed. 'Still, if you can't think of any other friends or family members who might be interested in avenging the bastard – might be worth taking a look at that list to see if anyone on it may somehow have found his way into the Red Castle.'

'Yes. Yes, but Terenti will deny he has it – it's going to take weeks to pry it out of the family's administration.'

He groaned, getting to his feet. 'Don't bother. I'll get it.'

'You – what?'

'As much as I'd appreciate spending a few weeks waiting for developments,' he said with a skewed grin at her, 'I'll get in trouble if I stay away from home that long. I'll have a word with the bastard. Give me a few hours and—'

'Runo,' she said, her voice too high. 'What are you planning to do?'

He looked a little too amused as he scratched the back of his head. 'Have a word with him? As I said?'

'You...' She stepped towards him, her lips struggling for words. As delightfully easy as it was, someone just solving her troubles for her – was he really going to *solve* them? 'If you kill my primary general I'll be in trouble, do you understand that? Slightly more trouble than I'm in now, if you need an indication of how much I don't want you to slit his—'

'Come on, Tamar,' he said. 'Do you think I survived twenty-five years in Raulinna by slitting every throat I didn't like?'

'No – but...'

Before she could finish that sentence he stood before her, hands on her upper arms, face dangerously close. The rest of her sentence froze in the back of her throat, her lips abruptly focussing on the nearness of his mouth rather than on the words they had been about to form. Why did he have to look so *confident*? So *capable*?

'Tamar.' Soft but stern, a voice that kindly commanded her to stop messing around. 'I'm not an idiot. Nobody's dying, and I'm getting you that list. Can you trust me on that, at least?'

Trust him. A Taavi assassin. Two days ago she would have laughed in his face and told her guards to get rid of him. Now –

I'd like to apologise.

In trouble. In so, so much trouble. But before she could stop herself, she nodded.

CHAPTER 15

W hy had she nodded?
  Why had he even asked her?
It was nonsense, Runo repeated to himself as he made his way through the Red Castle an hour and a good meal later. He was being nonsensical. He wasn't that kind of a man – a man to be trusted, a man who would heroically come to anyone's rescue. That type of work was meant for the people who actually gave a damn about the world, who were stupid enough to get attached to some noble goal and eventually ended up taking a sword in the heart for it. Not the kind of people who survived. The kind who didn't care. The kind to which he belonged –

To which he ought to belong, at the very least. Gods be damned. She may be bold and beautiful and vexingly human, and it didn't matter a whit – it *shouldn't* matter a whit. Not to the kind of man he was. Not to the kind of man the Empress trusted him to be.

Should have realised by now that reputations aren't always correct.

Oh, damn you, Tamar.

All of this was matter of necessity, he reminded himself at every corner he rounded. Staying alive. Finding that bloody traitor. She could trust him on that part indeed, because it was the part on which they agreed. She could also trust him to return to his mission after they found the man who wanted them both dead –

But he found himself hesitating at the door to Terenti's rooms. If the man had a list, if the traitor was indeed related to Anzor, the case might be solved within half an hour. Which would end this blissful truce before he had even made use of the key still spinning its tempting images at him from his pocket.

He knocked anyway. Tamar trusted him to find her traitor for her.

Terenti yanked open the door within seconds, then froze for at least a heartbeat – a heartbeat too long, Runo noted. He could have killed the man five times over in that frozen moment.

"*You?*'

'Evening,' Runo said, with his most amiable smile. 'Mind if I come in for a chat?'

'For a…' The man barked out a laugh with undeniable bloodlust. Anzor's brother, Runo recalled, and the thought hit him with a little too much rage. With no better idea of the late king's looks, his mind helpfully supplied him with the image of Terenti pressing hot candles against Tamar's bare arms – an image that gave him trouble remembering his promise not to kill anyone. 'A *chat*?'

'You know the concept, I presume?'

'She's gone mad,' Terenti groused, stepping forward from his doorway in the obvious expectation that Runo would clear the way for him. 'She can't just have you roam about without—'

Runo didn't move an inch. 'It's about Anzor's children.'

The other man froze. 'What?'

'I'd like to have a chat about Anzor's children.' He didn't lower his voice, deliberately so. The two servants passing by at the other side of the corridor would still be too far to make out his words, but Terenti was allowed to know he wouldn't change his tone even for any noble passers-by. 'So. Can I come in?'

'I know nothing about—'

'A shame – then I'll have to ask your queen about the matter. Sounds like the more time-consuming path, but if that's what you prefer—'

'Wait, wait,' Terenti snapped. 'What do you mean, asking Tamar…'

'Care to let me in, brother?'

For a moment the man only stared at him, his broad mouth set in a furious grimace. Then, abruptly, he stepped back and held open the door, clearly suppressing the urge to slam it shut in Runo's face.

'And?'

Runo gently closed the door behind himself and threw a look around. Sparsely furnished room, except for the lavish banner above the hearth, a fearsome boar against a dark green background. Well. Enough family pride to accommodate a boatload of brotherly embarrassment, indeed.

'As I said,' he said, sticking his hands into his pockets and ambling towards the window, deliberately ignoring the chair Terenti pointed out for him. It never failed to get on people's nerves. 'Anzor's children.'

'He and Tamar didn't have children.'

Runo rolled his eyes. 'Anzor's bastards, if you will. I'm looking for a list.'

'Doesn't exist.'

'Are you very sure about that, brother?'

'Listen here,' Terenti snapped, his face reddening. 'I don't know what pretty stories you told Tamar to make her keep you alive, because *I* surely would have had you hanged days ago – but you're not convincing me, do you understand? Even if the bloody list existed, a Taavi assassin would be the last person to see it. Anything else I need to clarify before I kick you out of this room?'

'A son of Anzor is trying to kill her,' Runo said.

More confidence than he felt, admittedly, but doubting in the face of this bastard wouldn't do.

Terenti's jaw went slack at once, a sight that would have been amusing if he'd been in a mood for amusement.

'Beg your pardon?'

'The man who hired me,' Runo said patiently, 'and incidentally, the man who shot three arrows at my face in the dark of night, was related to Anzor. So I'd like to know...'

'Why in the bloody world would any of Anzor's children kill *her*?'

'Oh, succession.' An effortless lie. Not that he should have lied – spreading the word about her husband's murder would be the quickest way to have chaos descend upon her court, and quite likely the easiest way to kill her. But he still had something like professional pride. He wasn't going to end her in roundabout ways, and he *definitely* wasn't going to rat on her for the justified murder of a man who already got out too easily. 'A son of the king would have a claim to the throne.'

Terenti stared at him. 'What madness is this?'

'Madness he told me himself,' Runo said, throwing out another lie. Terenti sucked in a sharp breath.

'You've known this all this time?'

'Thought I could still get out easily.' He shrugged. 'Then the issue with the gold arose, and I decided I should make some work of finding the bastard first. Why do you think Her Majesty allowed me to roam about like this?'

Terenti looked away. The mention of Tamar's title alone seemed to slap the sense back into him.

'Tamar knows this, I suppose?'

'Not yet.'

'What?'

'I'm trying to fix this without too much publicity,' Runo said, giving him another helpful smile. The confusion on the other's face alone was nearly worth those fifty pieces of gold. 'I don't like to draw attention. Can imagine the same is true for you. If you could just give me a list, I'll quietly find your traitor, everybody happy. But if such a list doesn't exist indeed...' He whistled out his breath. 'Well, I'll have to tell your queen all I know. Which will undoubtedly end with a general search for your murderous nephew and an entire kingdom aware of your failure to keep an eye on the little pest. Unpleasant, if you ask me. But if it's necessary...'

Something twitched at Terenti's temple. 'And why would I trust you?'

'Why wouldn't you?'

'For all I know you're not here to kill Tamar at all. You may be looking for the boy for some reason. You may be here to create chaos and instability at the court. You may—'

Runo sniggered. 'Do I strike you as the kind of man for five-layered plans?'

'You're a Taavi.'

Cuvrian, really – a correction he hadn't thought of for years. He didn't say it.

'And you were born in Redwood,' he said, 'but I'm not seeing much of the proverbial hospitality either. So perhaps you should forget about national reputations for a moment and just listen to what I'm telling you now – I'm offering you a chance to keep things simple. Your only chance. I'm not going to give you two of them, with my own life on the line. So what is it going to be?'

Terenti stared at him for a heartbeat or five – green-brownish eyes, blinking with a viciousness that again reminded Runo of those candle burns far too sharply. Then the man stood up straight and groused, 'May have something for you.'

'Wonderful. I just love sensible people.'

With a glare, Terenti snatched a keyring from his pocket and stepped to the door in the room's left wall. The lock creaked like a dying animal – not a door that was opened with any regularity. Behind it lay a small personal archive, parchment bulging from drawers and piles of books rising to near the ceiling. Under all the impressive iron and leather, Terenti's broad shoulders seemed smaller between that mass of information – more comfortable with swords than with ink, indeed. Still the search didn't take more than five minutes.

'Here's the best list I have,' the man groaned, turning around with a few sheets of parchment between his thick fingers. 'Never really paid much attention to it, to be honest. The secretaries handled all of it.'

Runo raised his eyebrows and accepted the parchment Terenti pressed into his hand. The other didn't meet his gaze. With the first glance at the list, the embarrassment made sense – the names, dates and locations filled three full pages.

'Fascinating,' Runo said. He couldn't help himself – out of anger or just to get under the man's skin, he wasn't sure. 'One wonders where he found the time to play king if—'

"*Very* careful now, Taavi.'

He shrugged and let his eyes glide over the list of names. It could hardly be one of the more recent children – the full page of progeny Anzor fathered in the twelve years of his marriage. The man sitting at that tavern table hadn't been a twelve-year-old boy, at least. Further down, then. Children all through Redwood, and some over the borders too, a nearly infinite stream of names that told him nothing. He flipped the last page. Terenti was holding his breath next to him, too tense to even curse.

Osanna, daughter of Dinah. Keran, son of Lousine. Simar, daughter of Eteri. Finally, the very last name on the list –

Runo blinked.

Then blinked again.

Then closed his eyes.

An explosive understanding and a violent dread flooded him simultaneously – Tamar's key. Her seal. Her letters. The arrows shot into his prison cell and the traitor knowing exactly how much she was keeping him alive.

'Good gods,' Terenti muttered beside him. 'Oh, good gods – I had no idea...'

Runo flicked the parchment aside, a white-hot alarm bursting through his veins. He barely heard the rest of Terenti's sentence, words of bland, useless shock.

Tamar, his mind screamed. Nobody's dying. *Trust me*. His feet were already moving, his fingers already searching for his knife – if the bastard had any idea what he knew, any idea what he *could* know, it might be a matter of minutes.

'What do we do?' Even Terenti sounded nearly frightened now. 'Do we tell her?'

'Tell the guards,' Runo snapped, striding towards the door. 'Make sure he isn't getting out of the castle unnoticed – make sure he can't reach his pretty friends in town. Can you handle that much, at least?'

'I'm not an *idiot*, Taavi!'

'Kind of you to clarify it. Wouldn't have known otherwise.' He slammed open the door. 'The guards, will you? I'm after the rest.'

CHAPTER 16

Tamar stared at the words under her fingers, her breath catching in her throat. Around her, echoing through her bedroom, she could still hear that golden voice – *Turned out the grain was poisoned.*

She had heard the story indeed.

She had remembered the details correctly.

Just a little paragraph in the third chronicle she opened, the last of the pile she'd hauled into her bedroom as the sky outside began to darken. No more than three lines of writing, deceptively dry and far too businesslike for the horrors that hid below the words – but they left no doubt about the events that had led to the massacre.

Good gods.

What was she supposed to *tell* him?

In a rush of agitation she grabbed for the two other books, threw them open on her blankets, and browsed to the index in the back. Now that she had a name, it was much easier. Sidra. There, the first almanac did mention the tragedy after all – a lousy throwaway sentence. No miracle she missed it on her first quick scan, but even that lousy sentence told her all she needed...

Someone knocked on her door.

Her heart shot into her throat – Runo? But no, he still had the key to the second door. He wouldn't confront her guards if he could as well walk in without the hassle. Amiran? Unlikely, at least until she sent him an apology for her irritation of that morning. Terenti, to complain about the assassin she set after him?

The door opened before that thought could even begin to concern her.

But it wasn't Terenti who came stepping in without waiting for her confirmation, or Amiran, or even Runo. Instead –

'Gocha?'

He shut the door behind him without an answer, his shoulders hunched, his gaze stubbornly focussed on the floor. Only at the click of the lock did he say, 'Your Majesty?'

'Is there anything wrong?' She tossed her books aside and shoved to the edge of the bed. 'Any news on—'

'What's the assassin doing around Terenti's room?' he blurted out, his voice too shrill.

Tamar stared at him. Eyes still avoiding her gaze, shoulders shaking. Fingers clenching and unclenching around his sword hilt. No *Your Majesty*, no *If I may ask*. She had seen him nervous before, but not like this – not as if he could collapse into hysterical panic any moment. Was he this worried about *Terenti*?

'He's looking into a few clues on the traitor,' she said, as calm as she could muster with the small sparks of unease firing through her guts. Why in the world would Gocha care much about Terenti's safety? 'But there's no need to worry, nobody's going to—'

'Why Terenti?'

'What?'

'Why would Terenti know about anything?'

Tamar stared at him, the unease thickening to a discomfort too strong to ignore. 'Gocha, are you—'

'No,' he snapped, knuckles whitening around his sword hilt. 'No, I'm not fine at all – why *Terenti*?'

You're overstepping, she'd have said two days ago. Don't be nonsensical – I know what I'm doing, and it's not your place to doubt my decisions. But he was all but trembling, up to the very tip of his thin nose, and was this really the moment to play Iron Queen again?

'It seems this case may have something to do with Anzor,' she said, closing her eyes for the shortest moment. 'Terenti should know more about his family affairs. So don't worry, we'll figure out soon enough...'

She didn't finish her sentence. Gocha shuffled back, moving to leave her room without as much as a greeting. But he didn't open the door to the corridor outside. Instead his hand came up and found the key still sticking in the lock, turned it shut with an apathetic, nearly mechanical gesture. His eyes still didn't swerve away from the floor.

'Gocha?'

The silence seemed colder all of a sudden, emptier. He drew a deep breath, and it sounded like the breath of a man preparing to jump off a cliff without knowing where he would land. The words caught in the back of her throat. The door. He'd locked the door. Why would anyone lock the door except...

"*Gocha*.'

He looked up.

For the first time since he had appeared on the doorstep of the Red Castle three years ago, freezing and exhausted and close to starvation, she met his eyes.

Eyes she knew.

That infinitely familiar brownish green, the colour of old moss, filled with a gleam that didn't fit his young face at all – something sharp, something vicious, a meanness of which the sight alone sent a prickling sensation over the scarred skin on her upper arms. Sungarden eyes.

Anzor's eyes.

She sat frozen on the edge of her bed, her limbs abandoning her. Gocha. Who knew his way around her room and his way around the castle's cells. Who had tried to kill Runo as soon as he stormed into her room after that first attempt, and tried to keep them from speaking alone at all further occasions. Who had heard her tell Amiran how the assassin *must* know more, mere hours before that ridiculous sum was promised to whoever would kill him.

Who stood staring at her now with those narrowed green eyes, his upper lip curling, his hand still tensing around the hilt of his sword.

'Gocha.' The words formed themselves on her lips. 'Gocha, what in the world—'

'Shut *up*!' he bit out.

Tamar fell silent, shock rather than compliance. The boy – *Anzor's* boy – took a stiff step forward, clutching his sword, squinting at her as if a look alone could kill her.

Kill her.

She had to move, she knew. She had to run and find a weapon and save herself – but this wasn't the threat she'd expected. No sinister conspirators, no threatening warriors. Just a thin, trembling boy, glaring at her with an anger that looked learnt rather than felt, holding on to his weapon like he was drowning. A boy she had trusted. A boy she had *wanted* to trust.

'Gocha, please.' A senseless plea, and yet she couldn't help herself. 'Don't do this. You don't have to do this. Please, let me explain...'

'Explain?' A hard, shrill laugh fell over his lips. '*Explain*? You *killed* him, you bitch – you—'

'Not because I *wanted* to!'

'Oh, did someone force you?' Another step forward. Another one. 'He always told me you hated him. I knew it as soon as he died – you killed him in cold blood and now you're trying to act like you couldn't *help* it? You...'

'I had to save my own life – Gocha, please, I—'

'You murdered my *father*!' he shouted, his voice breaking, and it was that sound that shattered the numbness of her limbs at once. She jolted back over her bed, scrambled away from his sword, away from the hysteria in his voice. He barely seemed to notice. 'Wasn't it enough that my mother died? You had to kill the only parent I had left too? You had to... to...'

A strange anguish in his voice, a desperation, a frantic attempt to believe the words he was speaking himself – the only parent. Anzor. Tamar crawled back until her back hit the wall behind her bed, her mind reeling – Anzor had still been alive three years ago. He must have known, the day the boy arrived at the castle. He must have known when he told her to send the little bugger off into the cold again, they had soldiers enough, what was the sense in hiring a child no thicker than a broomstick?

'That's what you call a parent?' she managed through the haze of her pounding heart. 'He made you keep it quiet, didn't he? He made you hide who—'

'He'd have told the world eventually! He said he would!'

'Gocha...' She wanted to cry. She wanted to reach for him and hug him. 'Did he pay you? Is that where you got those fifty pieces of gold? Did he—'

'He didn't *pay* me!' His voice was rising higher and higher. 'He *gave* it to me! Because I was his *son*! Because he loved me! Just because *you* don't understand—'

'You think *I* don't understand?' she interrupted, biting out a laugh. 'After twelve years you think I don't know the kind of man he was – do you want to know what he did to me? What he did to all those women – what he did to your mother—'

'Don't you dare speak a word about my mother, you bitch!'

She stared at him as he stood in the middle of her room, panting and shaking, looking far, far younger than his eighteen years. The Iron Queen should be furious now. Furious, and coming up with ways to escape and put his head on a pole somehow. But as she met his eyes, so close to the eyes she had learned to fear over a decade ago, she only felt – sadness?

Bitch. Her. For giving him a bed and a job and an education – for *caring*. But had he ever known she cared? She hadn't showered him in gold and soothing words, or any words at all, really. She had just... been. Kept him alive. Kept her word. But she hadn't been outspoken about it – *so busy making people fear and respect you.*

Her heart shrivelled in her chest.

'Gocha...'

'Don't bother pleading,' he snapped, yanking his sword from its sheath. 'Only reason I didn't kill you myself was that I didn't want to get caught. But you'll get what you deserve, and if that worthless Taavi can't do it...'

The wall was so cold and so unyielding against her back. Tamar closed her eyes and sucked in a breath – 'Gocha, please...'

'Shut *up*!'

'You'll never make it out of the castle alive – you'll never...'

A hard, desperate laugh. 'Oh, don't worry about me, bitch. I'll blame that bloody assassin of yours and that—'

'That,' Runo's voice said, cutting through the hysteria with the most reassuring nonchalance Tamar had heard in her life, 'is probably the worst plan you've made so far, brother.'

CHAPTER 17

"**R** *Runo*!'
Why did she sound *relieved*?

He stepped forward, into the bedroom, holding onto the doorhandle with a little more force than he'd like to admit. His breath still struggled through his throat from his sprint up the stairs. But she was alive – with her back against the wall on the furthest corner of her bed, perhaps, but *alive* – and at that realisation alone, his heartbeat came down a little.

'Well,' he said.

Somehow his voice still clung to that familiar nonchalance, as if even the confusion roaring through him was a joke. He'd never felt less like joking since that rainy afternoon when the Empress spared his life. 'I'm a little late, I see?'

'Runo – for the gods' sake...'

Her eyes, staring at him with a frightened gleam of trust. Her heaving chest. Her soft fingers clawing into the blankets. And Gocha, damned Gocha, with that sword clutched in his trembling hands...

It was too much for his mind, too much and too sudden – choices he was not prepared to make. Options he had not dared to think about. A future he had simply decided to forget as long as it lay behind other, more urgent obstacles – but now it was here, staring at him through a desperate pair of hazel brown eyes, and his thoughts imploded under the disarray of it, the conflicting reflexes, the expectations, the *loyalties*.

He had to kill her.

He had to keep her safe.

He had to get out of here. He had to stay. He had to disarm the little rat and swing him out over the balcony , he had to keep his promises – but *which* promises? *Kill the Iron Queen, Runo.* And yet –

Trust me.

'Runo?'

Oh, for hell's sake – why had she listened?

'No,' Gocha stammered, cowering away from him. 'No – what – where are you coming from – you—'

'From your uncle,' Runo said with a smile he didn't feel. 'Sends his regards, and probably his hangmen, by the time he gets his hands on you. Step away from that bed, will you?'

For a moment he hoped, more than anything he'd hoped in his life, that the boy wouldn't obey, that he would grab this last moment to attack – because at least an attack would give him an excuse to jump in and save Tamar's life without thinking through the consequences. Perhaps Gocha read the threat in his eyes. He shrunk back with little more than a hissed curse, although his cramped fingers around his sword hilt didn't relax in the slightest.

Runo closed his eyes, just for a fraction of a moment. The room was quiet enough to hear Tamar's quick breathing on the bed, Gocha's audible swallowing. Apart from them, only the pounding of his own heartbeat broke the silence.

And now?

Kill the Iron Queen.

Trust me.

'Runo,' Tamar whispered, and the sound of her voice sent claws tearing through him – his name on her lips, enough to remind him of the sweetness of her kisses, of the laughter breaking through on her face, of the sudden hope in her eyes. Seeing something about him he had never fully seen himself. *Not everything is a joke to you, then*. Oh, gods be damned, he might as well accept it –

He didn't want to kill her.

For hell's sake.

This was the kind of thought he should have forgotten before it even came up in his mind – the kind of thought that put people's heads on poles at home.

But there was no un-thinking it, and no denying it either. He knew the truth of it in the marrow of his bones, had perhaps known it since the first time she gave herself over to his touches – he didn't want to kill her. He didn't want her to die at all.

And yet... the Empress.

'Listen.' The words fell over his lips without thought, his mind's last desperate attempt to look even minimally composed. 'We had a deal, alright? I promised I'd keep you alive until we found the little bastard. Now we've found him, agreed? Not entirely according to plan, but you can't deny that we—'

'No.' Her voice grew stronger. 'No, you're not going to—'

'So it really doesn't matter much,' he interrupted, opening his eyes. If he got it over with fast enough, he might at least convince himself. 'I can kill him now, sure. And then what? You still have to die. I told you I wouldn't change my mind on that. So what's the difference if I stand back now and let him – do what he wants to—'

"*Kill* me.'

'Look, *I* don't want to do it!' he burst out, slamming the door shut behind him as he took one step forward into the room. In the edge of his sight he saw Gocha jolt back; Tamar didn't move, staring back at him with burning brown eyes. 'Happy now? I don't want to touch you with a finger, but if I want to live you still have to die, and this lousy bastard here is apparently itching to arrange exactly that – so can't we compromise? You die in the reassuring knowledge that I'll kill his ratty arse in the most unpleasant way I can imagine, and I...'

'Hey!' Gocha snapped, so indignant it would have been comical in any other situation. 'I'm still here!'

'That's not a bloody *compromise*, Runo!'

'It's all I can do!' Was he pleading now? What was he waiting for – for her to understand? For her to *agree*? 'What do you expect from me? To fling this little traitor of yours out of the window and kiss you goodbye and...'

"*Kiss*?' Gocha shrieked.

'...and ride back home for the Empress to kill me anyway? To sacrifice myself for you like some heroic idiot? Is that the kind of compromise you'd rather suggest?'

Panting silence. Gocha was looking back and forth between them, disgust growing on his face. Tamar didn't avert her gaze as she sat there in her blankets, on the bed where he should have joined her tonight – where he *wanted* to have joined her tonight. The look on her face was not a look of fear. Rather something like – pity? A look like she might well forgive him for the knife clutched between his fingers?

His resolve wavered. Far away, Gocha started, 'What do you mean, *kiss* her...'

'Runo,' she said, and the gravitas in her voice cut effortlessly through the boy's gabbling. Still she did not look away from him, didn't even blink. His name fell over her lips so carefully, such an unimaginable stability to her voice – a permanence, a safety he wanted to cling to more than he had ever wanted to cling to anything in his life. 'Runo, there's something you have to know – something I found...'

'Stop it!' Gocha blurted out. 'You can't just pretend I'm not here. You can't—'

'Runo – the Empress poisoned Sidra.'

He stared at her.

Loose syllables reached his mind, sticking together to words that refused to form a meaningful sentence. Empress. A word he knew. Poisoned. Another word. Sidra – had she said *Sidra*? She didn't know the name. He never told her the name. She couldn't know – Sidra. Poisoned. The Empress – poisoned...

'The *Empress,*' she repeated, as if he were a little child learning his language lessons. 'It wasn't the Cuvrian clans, Runo. It—'

Gocha lunged forward.

In the blink of an eye, reflexes kicked in.

Through the mist of bewilderment, through all rational, sensible objections, Runo moved before he decided to. She couldn't die now. She couldn't die with that sentence unfinished. Damn the little bastard with his damned father and his damned treason and his damned revenge – the fury exploded within him as he leapt towards the bed, knife hand coming up in the same movement. The world was reduced, for a fraction of an instant, to the boy's sword swinging down and Tamar's cry and the cold, reassuring weight of the weapon in his own hand. This, at least, was something he knew, something he could do. Old instincts took over, grained into his body by hours and hours of training. He clenched his hand around Gocha's iron-clad shoulder and jerked him closer, yanking both the boy and his sword away from Tamar. The point of the weapon missed her by mere inches. Runo moved before the other could recover, cool certainty washing over him. Arm around shoulders. Hand under chin. Fingers forcing up the boy's head, baring the uncovered neck below. Skin and arteries splitting open under the edge of his blade, a cascade of warm blood gushing from the wound.

Tamar cried out, and the smooth, thoughtless routine shattered to pieces.

He abruptly let go of Gocha's slackening body and staggered back, away from the dying boy, away from the bed, suppressing the urge to drop his stained knife and wipe the sticky blood off his palms and fingers. His breath rasped through his throat. Gocha's eyes stared back at him from the puddle of blood forming on the floor, young and empty and nothing like home anymore –

Nothing like Sidra.

Sidra.

Tamar flinched when he turned towards her. His reeling mind barely noticed.

'Repeat that,' he growled. 'What did you say about—'

'The Empress.' Even with shaking shoulders, with her eyes darting from the dead boy at his feet to his blooded knife and back to his face, her voice didn't waver. 'I told you I'd heard the story before. Your version of it – it didn't align with what I remembered. So I took a look at our chronicles and...'

Only now did she hesitate under his piercing glance. Chronicles. He hadn't paid attention to the books scattered over her bed. Were they the same books she had been reading this afternoon?

'It was never the Cuvrian civil war, Runo,' she continued, quieter now. 'The place lay in the middle of the Taavi frontline. They were the ones who needed that valley to break through the clans' defences...'

'No.'

'You were so young.' Why did she sound *apologetic*? 'Of course you didn't remember the details. Of course you believed whatever lies they told you afterwards – don't...'

'No,' he repeated. There was nothing else he could say. There was nothing else to his thoughts anymore. 'I – no. No. That's not—'

'Read it,' she interrupted, grabbling one of the books from her pillow. 'Here – page thirty-seven – it's all in there. This one too, page eighty – I'm sure I can find more of them, if you...'

He stared at the book she held out for him, a tingling sensation creeping up along his spine. The heavy cover looked like it might contain a nest of vipers if he opened it.

"*Read* it!' she repeated, more pressing now.

He staggered forward like a sleepwalker and snatched the book from her, the old leather clammy in his hands. Page thirty-seven. His fingers left bloodstains on the parchment as he browsed through the priceless, illuminated writing, and he couldn't muster the energy to care. Too much text for his brain to take in, but his eyes found the name halfway down page thirty-seven nearly immediately.

... the village of Sidra, situated at the pass to the Toril valley, held off the advance of the Taavi army for three months. On the 12th of Midsummer month, the besiegers sent bags of poisoned grain into the village. On the 18th of Midsummer month, the village was taken. No survivors were reported.

'No,' he heard his own voice say, from far, far away.

'This one, too.' She shoved the opened book into his hands before he could blink, and his eyes found the words with ruthless ease. *The siege of Sidra was broken by the Empire through a ruse with poisoned food, and the Taavi army progressed into the valley beyond by the end of Midsummer month.*

He closed his eyes. The books slipped from his hands with a dull thud he barely heard – the Toril valley. The Taavi army. Home. *No survivors.* Eyes staring back at him from the darkness of his memory, no longer just watching but accusing him – traitor, their looks said. The Taavi army. Had he killed for the wrong side – killed for *their* murderers?

'Runo,' Tamar said quietly. 'Runo, I don't blame you – you couldn't know—'

'Stop,' he managed. 'Please.'

But the silence wasn't better, or even any more silent – the silence screamed memories at him, his mother collapsing in the doorway of the hut, aunt Vara slumped forward in her chair, the empty-eyed toddlers in the sand of the square. That voice, that damned, honey-sweet voice – *he may live and serve us.*

Bile rose in his throat. He stepped back without knowing where he was going – away. Away from his own mind, away from this room, away from the shock, the confusion, the unbearable temptation of Tamar's voice so close to him. *Live and serve us.* Out, he needed to get *out* – silence and darkness and nothing else –

'Runo?'

He turned and started walking. The first steps were the hardest. Then it was just a matter of keeping to it. Door. Room. Door. Corridor. Out – *out.*

"*Runo*!'

The castle turned around him. His mind was a whirlpool. But his feet took over, a last reflex of self-preservation. With nothing else he could think of to do, he simply gave up, and ran.

CHAPTER 18

'Still no news?' a soft woman's voice said.

Tamar turned away from the pile of letters. Lady Zovinar of Tanglewood had appeared in the doorway of the study, her expression timid and cautious, but her gaze no less sharp for it. Over the last few days, Tamar had found the girl's frail exterior could be dangerously deceptive.

Her first impulse was to give a bland answer and leave the interaction at that. Zovinar would get the hint. Then again – did she have anything better to do? The letters formed a pile of dukes' seals, Androughan birch bark, an infinite amount of boring little notes, and nothing she'd been looking for. Nothing from the south. Nothing from Rock Hall, either.

As a matter of fact, the message she was looking for hadn't arrived for the last thirty-five days, and by now she began to doubt it would ever arrive at all.

'News?' she said.

'You've been in such a hurry to take a look at all arriving mail these days,' Zovinar said, a slight blush rising on her cheeks. 'I thought you were waiting for something.'

'Ah.' Deceptive, indeed. 'Yes. It's not here, I'm afraid.'

'I'm sorry to hear – is there anything I can do?'

The reflex was still there, that instinctive urge to raise her chin, straighten her shoulders, and curtly declare that she certainly did not need any assistance. But it was almost as easy now to sigh and say, 'Thank you. I can't think of anything now, but that's kind of you to offer.'

'Well, you've been really very helpful during this entire business.' The blush deepened to a bright red. 'I just wanted to say – if you don't mind...'

'Oh, no. Come in.'

The girl slipped into the room and closed the door behind her, with the quick, gingerly movements that made her look younger than her twenty-something years. Predictably, Rusuvan's defenders had focussed on that point during the court case of the last days – a silly little girl, just look at her, can we honestly convict a man based on the accusations of a woman who can't even keep her own words straight?

Except it turned out Zovinar *could* keep her words straight. Quiet and demure, perhaps, but unwavering for three full days of questioning and court proceedings.

'Take a seat,' Tamar added, sinking into her own chair. Even now, after a month, her body gave a little flutter whenever her eyes swerved over her desk – but at least she had learned to ignore the memory by now. 'Say what's on your mind.'

'I just wanted to make sure you weren't unhappy about it,' Zovinar said, sitting down. 'My request. I hope – after all the work you put into the case...'

'Oh, that was alright. Terenti came to his senses surprisingly quickly.'

Zovinar blinked. 'Did he?'

'Didn't I tell you? This set-up was his suggestion – that is to say, he suggested the compromise that the defence got extra speaking time, if I wanted to keep the judges.' Tamar shrugged. 'I think he hoped you would cave under the pressure. Since you're the one who didn't, I'd say you were fully within your rights to make any request you wanted.'

Zovinar smiled – still a little hesitant, but a smile like a sunrise nonetheless. 'Alright. Thank you.'

'Although you should realise...'

She paused, and Zovinar said, 'Rusuvan will likely flee to Copper Coast? Where Ulrick won't send him away because you didn't deliver Garreth to him either?'

'Ah. You thought that through already?'

'Yes, of course.'

Tamar raised her eyebrows. 'Then why did you ask the judges to keep him alive? Banishment isn't much of a punishment if he can just take up a luxury living at Ulrick's court.'

'Ulrick will have to stop bothering you about housing his exiles as soon as he allows Rusuvan into his home,' Zovinar said, nearly apologetically. 'I'd quite appreciate it if Garreth could come with me next time I'm visiting the Red Castle.'

Tamar leaned back in her chair, unable to suppress her smile. 'Ah. Clever.'

Zovinar blushed again. 'You really don't mind?'

'Not at all. At least this way Terenti can't accuse me of arranging the outcome of the case all along.' She shook her head, sighed. 'So – I can expect to finally meet your infamous exile of a husband soon?'

Again that bright smile, and for the shortest moment a feeling frighteningly close to envy set its claws into her heart. Zovinar would ride home after all this excitement and find a husband and an infant daughter waiting for her in Tanglewood Castle. Farmers and villagers who didn't need constant supervision. Guards who wouldn't be trying to kill her. While Tamar would spend her evenings ignoring Pridon's greedy glances and reading letters of people who had nothing of sense to say, or at least nothing about the man who stormed out of her castle a month ago and never showed a sign of life since.

Dead, probably, Amiran said. The criminals downtown must already have been on his trail before the news of their employer's death spread; with no income to gain from it anymore, they probably buried the body in the woods and forgot about it. Which was a reasonable theory, and it became all the more reasonable with every day that went by. If even Jaghar and Viviette couldn't find a trace of him, after she explicitly asked them to look out for him – then what were his chances?

'Your Majesty?'

She tore her thoughts away from the menacing images. 'Sorry, what did you say?'

'If there's anything else I can do for you now – I could ask the servants to bring you a cup of mulled wine? Or warm milk? That always helps me to sleep, at least.'

Sleep. It had been a long time since she last slept a full night. But she smiled, because it had also been a long time since anyone offered her a glass of warm milk, and said, 'That would actually be wonderful, thank you.'

'I'll arrange that, then,' Zovinar said as she stood up and nodded with sudden determination. 'And I'll probably see you tomorrow before I leave.'

'Yes, I'll make sure to see you off.'

The girl curtsied and hurried to the door, then turned again. 'And – Your Majesty?'

Tamar closed her eyes for a heartbeat. 'Just call me Tamar.'

'Oh – are you sure?'

'Of course.' She managed a smile. 'I can hardly go by Her Majesty, Queen Tamar of Redwood all the time, can I? What did you want to say?'

'Just...' Zovinar swallowed, then straightened her shoulders. 'Nothing much, really. I hope you get that letter soon.'

'Yes,' Tamar said, forcing down the bitter fear for what had to be the thousandth time in the past week alone. 'Thank you. So do I.'

CHAPTER 19

The building loomed up from the night, its contours drawn only by the absence of stars in the wall of black that stretched out before him.

Still Runo's feet found the way with ease. Over the cobblestones. Through the rusty gate that separated the marble walls from the dirty streets. Over the smooth paving that covered the last yards to the closed gate. Weeks of travelling, some of which had come close to killing him – and yet, now that he finally stood before his destination, he only felt a strange, calm certainty, a determination that hadn't come over him since the night he climbed onto Tamar's balcony to kill her. His steps didn't falter in those last yards. He climbed the five low steps to the gate and slammed the brass knocker against the wood three times, then waited for the sound of footsteps inside. His patience wasn't tested for long. Even in the depth of night, the guards didn't slack here.

The door was pulled open by a stocky young man whose frowning face looked even more sinister in the candlelight of his lantern. Runo didn't want to know what *he* looked like in that same light. His white shirt hadn't been white for weeks; a fight had torn his trousers, and he had stitched up the cut too hastily. It had been days since he'd last seen a mirror, and judging by the guards deepening scowl, he should be grateful for it.

'Name and reasons for visit?'

'Runo,' he said. 'Bronze corps.'

A frown. 'I've heard that name.'

'Well possible,' Runo said with a shrug. 'I've been here before. Not the first time the Empress has given me a job around this place.'

'A job in the depth of night?'

'I prefer not to make her wait. Would advise you the same, really.'

The guard snorted. 'Password, then?'

'Amaranthine.'

'Thanks. Come in.'

He followed the man into the building, where the occasional lantern threw a little light over the smooth marble walls and staircases. His eyes swerved to the right; the guard followed his look with another snort.

'You've been here before indeed, I see.'

'Won't need long,' Runo said. 'Do you have some light for me?'

A spare lantern was pulled from under a sturdy marble bench. Accompanied by only the flickering candlelight, he climbed the stairs to the second floor, the shadows dancing around him, his footsteps breaking through a wall of silence. Three doors and he reached the room he was looking for. When he turned the handle, the door swung open without a creak.

Shelves and shelves of books stared back at him from their dusty darkness.

He hesitated, no longer than a heartbeat. Then he lifted his lantern and stepped inside, navigating through the narrow aisles purely by memory – he had seen the sign at his last visit, *Cuvri War*, and hardly paid attention to it at that occasion. Yet he found it within minutes now, next to the sections on Omest, Gennekha, Beyond the Desert... All the former nations reduced to provinces these days. Their fight reduced to mere piles of paper in some stuffy marble rooms, their dead reduced to dry lists of names.

The light of his candle slid along the spines until he found what he was looking for – a shelf of chronicles bound in red leather, their names pressed into each cover in dusty gold.

The rightmost book said *The Cuvri War Under Maiva Ilmara*, and that was the book he took off its shelf. Then he sank down at the nearest reading table, put his lantern at the corner, rolled up his sleeves, and set to work.

It took him no more than five minutes to find it.

It took him fifteen minutes at least to read that one page, though.

He sat in the dead silence of night, a small cocoon of candlelight in the pitch dark of the archives, dead eyes reading along over his shoulders and whispering at him from the darkest cracks and corners of the room. Surrounded by that company, he drank in every word, every lie, a dozen times over, until he could read the words on the inside of his eyelids even when he closed his eyes. Until he could taste the shape of them on his tongue – the cold, metallic taste of fury.

Then he stood, tipped over the lantern, and walked.

He found the guard waiting for him at the foot of the stairs, looking even more suspicious than at his arrival. Before he could open his mouth, the man hissed, 'Runo, you said?'

His fist clenched around the knife in his pocket. 'How many times do you want me to introduce myself?'

'I *knew* I'd heard your name lately.' Sharp, undiluted triumph. 'They're looking for you in Raulinna. The Empress wants a word with you about a job you should have finished by now. I have orders not to let you out of sight until – *agh*...'

'Shame,' Runo said, driving the blade another inch deeper into the man's chest, then pulling it back just as abruptly.

The lifeless body slid to the floor, lantern clattering to smithereens on the marble. Through the cracked glass the burning oil seeped out, and the flames drew eerie lines of fire on the smooth white floor.

'Wanted to ask you to pass on a message,' Runo added as he turned for the door and threw a last glance over his shoulder. 'But this will probably get the point across too.'

Then he was out, back into the cold night, his fingers still tight around his knife. Behind him the silhouette of the archive building was no longer as dark as half an hour ago, the first flames lighting the rooms behind the windows. Runo barely heard the cries of alarm echoing through the city. While the guards rushed closer, he found his way out as easily as he'd come in, back to the grasslands surrounding the place, back to the stolen horse waiting for him. With the words of that cursed chronicle still etched into his eyes, his mind didn't seem capable of forming more than a single thought –

Tamar.

Tamar.

CHAPTER 20

*D*ear *Viviette*, Tamar wrote.

Then she hesitated, pen hovering above the parchment. Not because she didn't know what to write, but rather because she wasn't sure what *not* to write. How often could she repeat the question before it would turn her from mildly obsessed into an utter madwoman? One day she'd have to stop, and yet...

She dipped her pen in the ink before she could change her mind. *Once again – I suppose you didn't hear anything from the Empire yet?* Or from the slums of Redwood, she added in thought. From the many Riverlands villages lying in between her kingdom and the Empire itself. But that point at least she'd made often enough; Viviette would understand the full question even if she didn't spell out every word of it.

Apart from that, she wrote on, scraping herself together, *I have some more recent notes on...*

Something clicked behind her.

A soft metallic click, sounding suspiciously like the lock that hadn't been open for a month and a half.

Tamar froze in her seat, her pen halted mid-word. So she was going crazy after all. Hearing sounds that weren't there – now she only needed to start hallucinating and she'd be well on her way to turn into the kind of mad queen that ended up locked into a tower for her own safety.

'Tamar?'

The madness forgotten, she jerked around.

He was standing in the doorway, unsmiling. Dark curls dripping from the spring rain. Twigs sticking to his muddied clothes. Fingers clenched around the small iron key.

Alive.

Tamar rose from her chair, slowly, feeling like she could sink through her knees any moment. When she opened her lips, no sound came out – her voice abandoned her under those sharp golden eyes that had haunted her dreams for weeks on end. Before she could gather her wits, he stepped inside and pulled the door shut behind him. Even as he nodded at the key in his hand, he didn't take his eyes off her.

'You didn't change the lock.'

'I – no.'

'Good gods. Stupid or suicidal?'

She opened her mouth again, with equally little result. It was him, it *really* was him, ambling into her room after all these weeks as if mere days had gone by since he stormed out of her castle without even a coat on his shoulders. Still muscular and handsome and insufferably nonchalant, and yet...

Yet *something* had changed about him – dulled the twinkle in his eyes, soured his smile. She swallowed. Was she stupid? Or suicidal?

'Just – just sentimental, I'm afraid.'

'Really?' He stuck the key back into his pocket and folded his arms, a mirthless grin on his face. 'Missed the nostalgic sensation of a knife to your throat?'

'Hell's sake, what do you – you have no idea...' She sucked in a breath. 'I've been *worried* about you! Where in the world have you—'

'*Worried*?' His grin faded. 'Why would you worry about *me*?'

'The state you stormed out of here! I thought you might throw yourself off a rock somewhere!' Her voice was rising, six weeks of fear and frustration welling up in her. 'You can't just disappear for months after I shocked you into saving my life and then expect me *not* to worry about...'

Runo's eyes were wide with incomprehension. 'I tried to kill you that night!'

'Pretty miserable attempt, wouldn't you say?'

He burst out laughing, a bitter, joyless laugh. 'Tamar, what are you doing? You're supposed to scream your heart out and call your guards, not start fussing about whether I wore my scarf in the cold and ate my vegetables while—'

'Do I need to scream?' she interrupted, and he fell silent, blinking at her. Something really *was* different about his expression. If he had been any other man, she might have called it a glimpse of insecurity.

'What?'

'Were you planning to hurt me?'

'Of course I'm not bloody planning to hurt you, but you're not supposed to *trust* me all of a—'

'Then you're the one who's fussing here.' She closed her eyes, rubbing her temples. 'Sit down, good gods. Dry your hair, you'll catch a cold this way. Tell me where you've been.'

He did not sit down. He did not dry his hair. He said, 'Noviisa.'

Tamar stared at him. Noviisa. The *Empire*? 'What in the world were you...'

'Reading military reports.'

Her heart skipped. 'Oh.'

'Not that I distrust you.' He gave her another wry smile. 'Then again, I suppose I did. A little. At least I considered the option that your scribes just wrote down rumours rather than the true history of that war. You people have a tendency to blame everything on the Taavi in this part of the world.'

He kept silent, staring at the floor before his feet. The raindrops were still slipping from his dark hair, the only thing moving around him. Tamar didn't dare to speak.

'But of course,' he said eventually, 'you're hardly doing so without a reason, are you?'

'Did they...'

'Their books said what you said. What your library said. That it was their own bloody army.' His voice grew sharper, louder. 'They presented it as a *victory*, the bastards – threw poison into a bag of grain and waited and called it a victory when everyone...'

She stared at him as he stood there, trembling, clenching his fists and shoulders. Then he deflated, as quickly as the fury had risen in him, sagged back against the wall and closed his eyes. His breath struggled in his throat in short, little inhalations.

'I never – even – *questioned* them.'

'You were seven!'

He made a disparaging gesture. 'I grew older.'

'You were surviving.'

'Is that an excuse to be a slavish idiot?'

'There's nothing slavish about being loyal,' she said sharply. 'It turns into slavishness only if you stay around when you find out the loyalty is unjustified, and you don't give the impression...'

She paused, suddenly afraid of the question she was about to ask. But he grinned when he looked up at her – a grin that suggested he might set his teeth into someone's throat any moment.

'Oh, don't worry. I'm not going back.'

'You're – not?'

'Of course I'm not. Maiva can go fuck herself.' He shrugged. 'Not going to kill you either, in case that wasn't clear.'

'That – that was clear.'

'Good. Glad to hear.'

She had no idea what to do with her limbs as she raised her hands, lowered them again, clenched her fingers into a fist and released them. The sight of him alone, rumpled and messy as he was, woke up far too many of the feelings that had kept her awake for nights on end. Not going to kill her. A dangerous warmth curled through her body, seeping through her skin in every place his gaze could touch.

'So...' Deep breath. Straight spine. 'If you're not going to kill me – what exactly are you doing here?'

'Thanking you,' he said, shrugging. 'And asking if you need anyone around to slash a couple of throats for you every now and then.'

Her breath caught. 'What?'

'I'm offering you my services, Tamar,' he said, sliding onto the floor with his back against the wall. His grin still didn't pass the bar of lukewarm. 'If you have any use for me. Will gladly kick some of your so-called guards from your room – or whatever else you need from me. You're the queen. I'll be happy to take instructions.'

'Happy to...' Her voice shot up half an octave. 'Instructions? *You*?'

'Thought I might as well try something different in life.'

'Runo, are you *alright*?'

'Of course I'm not.' Another one of those mirthless laughs that made her heart cramp up. 'I thought I could be certain of a single thing, and it turned out to be the biggest lie of all – am I supposed to be *alright* about that?'

'No – no, but—'

'But don't worry,' he interrupted, looking away. 'Just give me my regular meals and a bed to sleep in and I'll be fine. I don't need much.'

She stared at him, sitting small and rain-drenched against her bedroom wall. Had she ever thought she wanted him to stop being so infuriatingly careless about everything – had she ever wanted him to become *this*?

'Even if you don't need much, surely there's more you'd like to—'

'Tamar, leave it be.' He rested the back of his head against the wall, closing his eyes. 'I've survived worse.'

'I don't doubt you'll survive, but it would be nice if you did a little better than that.'

'Why would you care?'

'You saved my life, for a start.'

'From myself, yes,' he said, looking up with a joyless chuckle. 'Do you realise I could have killed you just as easily?'

'I don't think you could have, to be honest.'

'Tamar...'

'And it's not just that – do you have any idea what you did to me?' At once the words poured out, six weeks of fear and frustration breaking free. 'All these things you told me... No one else would have been mad enough to be that honest with me, and I'm beyond grateful you were. I've been trying to keep it in mind, all of it. I'm doing better. Still nowhere near perfect, but...' She sucked in a breath, her clenched fists suddenly trembling. 'Better. So...'

So tell me what you want, she had planned to say. Tell me what you need. Tell me you won't truly take up the life of the dutiful soldier and treat me as your almighty queen, because I still don't want you any more pliable. But the words escaped her under his look, a gleam flickering back to life in his eyes like the last stubborn embers of a dying fire. A look that reminded her, gently and painfully at once, of the way he had looked at her as she came in his arms all those weeks ago.

A nearly invisible smile hovered at the corners of his lips – a smile so hopeful, yet so cautious that her heart skipped a beat, then pounded on too fast.

'I hadn't dared to hope that much,' he said quietly.

She managed a laugh. 'You thought you'd just find the good old Iron Queen here? After all that happened – after all you said?'

'I was prepared for the possibility, at least.'

'And yet you came back.'

He made a gesture at himself as if to say, as you see. Tamar sank down in her chair with another breathless laugh, her mind spinning.

'The good old Iron Queen *would* have arrested you at first sight, do you realise that?'

'Of course I do.'

'And yet...'

'I wanted to see you again,' he said, his voice flat with the simplicity of it. 'You really shouldn't underestimate how much I wanted to see you again.'

Her heart made good attempts to escape her chest now, pounding against her ribs with such force she feared the bones might break. 'To thank me?'

'To...' He sucked in a breath. 'To know you were true.'

She blinked. 'What do you...'

'I don't think you understand what a strange phenomenon you are to me, Tamar,' he said, avoiding her gaze. 'I'm not sure you can ever fully understand. Just – the only kind of honour I've known in my life is the kind they sport in Raulinna, where they swear fealty to their lords and plot to murder them in the same breath, where they swear to protect the weak and fuck farmers' children the day after. And then there's you.' An unfocussed gesture at her. 'With your bloody integrity and your bloody word and your bloody *everything*, and none of it makes sense to me. But I *want* to understand it, do you see? Even if I had to learn it from your cells. Even if it were the last thing I did in life. I just want to know...'

Another moment of hesitation. Then, sitting up a little straighter, he finished, 'That it exists. That you are what I thought you are.'

She was nothing but a heartbeat now, felt the rhythm of it in the very tips of her toes and fingers. 'So – if I give you my word I'm not throwing you into any cells again...'

For a fraction she hesitated, her lips already parted – a fraction of a heartbeat in which the universe itself seemed to hang suspended, stars and moon halting their circles in anticipation of her question. A question from which she knew there would be no coming back, no unhearing the answer... But she wanted that answer. She craved it like a flower craving the autumn rains, a hunger rising from a depth of her that only he had seen.

'Then what do you want?'

He looked up, eyes meeting hers without a hint of hesitation or uncertainty. The look of a man prepared to die for the truth on his lips.

'You,' he said.

Her.

She felt her lips move, but no sound came out. Her. Just now, she wanted to say, just this night? Or do you mean – could you mean – that you dreamt of me as much as I dreamt of you? That you'll stay here, that you'll want me time and time again and keep the weight of the world off my shoulders? That you'll continue making everything so ridiculously easy?

Ten feet away from her, Runo smiled, and for the first time the lights returned to his eyes – those lights that told her he was about to be insufferably annoying again. She had never imagined she could be so happy to see them.

'Shocked the words out of you?'

A laugh fell from her lips. 'What – what exactly do you mean...'

His smile turned brighter. 'Need details?'

'No – I mean...'

'I want to tear that bloody dress off you, Tamar,' he said, holding her gaze, searching for her reaction. 'I want to hear you beg for me. I want to throw you over that bed and fuck you until you're crying out my name, and then I want to fall asleep holding you and fuck you awake again in the morning. I frankly haven't wanted much else for weeks, and I don't think I'll stop wanting it anywhere soon either. Enough detail, or do you want me to continue?'

She had trouble breathing all of a sudden, her mouth turning dry under the challenge in his eyes. With rekindled vigour he leaned forward, arms resting on his knees, grin broadening.

'And now you're supposed to say something about the damned impertinence,' he added helpfully. 'About how you'll have me – I don't know, quartered? Thrown into boiling oil? Quartered *and* fried?'

There was no stopping the laugh rising in her. 'You know very well I have no intentions to quarter you.'

'No?' he said, pulling up his eyebrows. 'It's going to be the boiling oil, then?'

'Good gods. If you go on like this I might well be tempted.'

'Thankfully,' he said dryly, 'avoiding your death sentences is one of my more exceptional talents. I have all faith I can persuade you to be a little milder.'

Persuade her. Oh, gods. Any moment she expected the flames to come bursting through her skin now. But she'd be damned if she made it *that* easy for him – so she stood up, took a step back, and said, 'It really is a miracle how quickly you can bounce back into arrogance, do you know that?'

He laughed, getting to his feet in a single, supple movement. 'It's easy to get arrogant when you look at me like that.'

'Like what?'

'Like you missed me.'

With three steps he stood before her, the distance between their bodies reduced to a magnetic, smouldering few inches. Her knees turned to pulp at that sudden imminence. Even through the sweat and rain he still smelled like himself, that rich scent of southern spices – a scent of freedom.

'Miss you?' she managed somehow. 'A man like you?'

Runo chuckled, raising his hand to her face. There his fingers hesitated, hovering so close that she could feel the warmth of them on her cheek.

'Still a terrible liar,' he said softly. 'But a beautiful one, too.'

Her limbs wouldn't move in anticipation of his touch. The presence of his hands alone reduced her to little more than a puppet at his strings, a body obeying his mind before it obeyed her own – even her voice no longer found its way over her lips. Please, she wanted to say. Do what you want to do, then. Make me forget myself. Make me...

A shiver ran through her. Make me lose control.

A smile played around the corners of his mouth. It was too knowing, that smile, and too damn meaningful, looking straight through her again. Now finally he touched her cheek, sending bolts of lightning through her. Trailed his fingertips along her jaw with butterfly-soft insistence. Curled around her chin and made her hold his gaze, honey-coloured eyes and that smile that invited her to forget the world forever.

'Don't be scared, Tamar.'

'I'm not scared,' she breathed. 'I'm just – not very sensible around you.'

'I know.' His voice was a song, twisting and turning into every quiet corner of her mind. 'It's alright. You don't have to be.'

She closed her eyes and inhaled his scent, unable to think straight. She didn't have to be. Not for him. Not with him. The surge of relief made her feel like fainting, a drunk, dizzy sensation – but with his body so close, his arms ready to catch her, she couldn't be bothered to worry even about her knees giving in.

'I've missed you,' she whispered.

His hand slowly let go of her chin. She still felt his gaze on her face, setting every inch of her on fire; when she opened her eyes, he was observing her with soft, cautious eyes as if she would go up in smoke if he made one wrong move too many.

The whole world felt like it could crumble around her any moment, too – like a dream that had to end soon. Too strange to be real. Too good to be real. But she raised her hands to his chest, her heart fluttering as if it were the first time she touched him, and under the rain-drenched linen of his shirt he was undeniably warm and firm and real against her fingertips.

Again she shivered, despite the fire burning in the hearth behind her. His smile grew a shade more wicked.

'Go ahead, Your Majesty.'

Was it a command? A request? A grant of permission? She couldn't muster the effort to care, to force a single more sensible thought about the madness of this night. With careful fingers she began to unfasten his shirt, button by button, revealing the body she'd never even seen naked before. A chest as muscular as she'd known from its shape under her fingers. An equally masculine abdomen. A thin trail of dark curls running down from his navel, growing broader where it disappeared below the band of his trousers. Runo didn't move as her hands wandered down along his torso, watching her silently until she loosened the last of his buttons. Then he quickly tugged the shirt off his shoulders. A pair of strong, tanned arms, and on the left –

A row of small lines inked into his lower arm, arranged in groups of five, like dark blue scars against his olive-coloured skin.

Her breath caught as she ran a fingertip over the marks, counting even though she didn't want to count. Forty-two. Her finger paused at the empty spot just after the last line.

'That should have been me,' she said quietly.

He slowly breathed out. 'Yes.'

She looked up. A wistful gleam had risen in his eyes, but he didn't pull his arm from her grip, didn't look away. That deep, golden look – the eyes of the man who told her about the horrors of his childhood in the silence of the night rather than the man who burst into her room with a knife in his hand.

She looked down, brushed her thumb over the marks a last time, then pulled his arm to her face and pressed her lips against the inked skin. He stiffened. When she let go and met his gaze again, his eyes were burning.

'You...' An incredulous smile flickered around his lips. 'Oh, Tamar. You signed your own fate there, I'm afraid.'

'What fate do you...'

He lowered his head before she finished, warm lips brushing over her forehead, her eyebrow, her cheek. Only half an inch away from her mouth did he pause, breathing quietly against her lips.

'This one,' he muttered.

And kissed her.

She had been prepared, and yet she wasn't – not for the overwhelming tenderness of his kiss, the strength, the passion, the inevitability of it. His lips held her captive, mesmerizing her with every twist and turn, drawing quiet moans from her whenever they released her for even a fraction of a moment. His strong fingers around the back of her head drew her closer. His arm around her waist pinned her against his firm torso, his hardening arousal pressing into her lower belly. Tamar wrapped her arms around his shoulders and found his broad back under her fingers, unmovable as a rock even when she clawed her nails into his skin. He groaned, then opened his mouth to her to meet the cautious invitation of her tongue. Her knees gave in. Had he not still held her around her waist, she might have collapsed at his feet.

He breathed a chuckle as he pulled back and gently nibbled her lower lip. 'Surrendering already?'

'Was it ever much of a fight?' she muttered.

'Hardly,' he admitted, flashing her that quick, wicked smile. His free hand drew burning lines over her neck and shoulders, to the edge of her bodice, the fragile ribbons holding it shut. One yank and her corset fell open, releasing her breasts. 'Won't keep me from claiming my victory, though.'

'Still such an arrogant—'

His kiss drowned the rest of her words, and it was a kiss that didn't allow any objection, any sensible thought. With two steps he pushed her towards her waiting bed. Tamar clawed her fingers into his bare shoulders the moment she felt the mattress in the back of her knees, and he allowed her to pull him along into the blankets. Limbs intertwining, kisses growing wilder, they fell into the soft silk and wool where he had pinned her down so much more violently weeks ago –

where she had held a knife to his throat on that very first evening.

She pulled from his embrace and pressed her lips to the vulnerable skin just below the stubble of his beard, tasting him with a flick of her tongue. Runo groaned and rolled her on her back, tearing down her bodice with an unmistakable hunger in his eyes.

'Any knives I have to watch out for tonight, Your Majesty?'

She fell back in her pillows with a breathless laugh. 'Thought you had enough faith in your abilities to escape my death sentences?'

'Fair point,' he muttered, pressing his lips to her collarbone, then grazing down to the onset of her breast. 'Allow me to try, then...'

If she had still planned to reply, all sense and speech abandoned her the moment he closed his lips around her nipple and gently sucked at it. His fingers found her other breast and wrapped around it, thumb stroking the nipple as he flicked his tongue over the other, sending fierce flares of aching need through her. With an uncontrollable moan she arched into his caresses, pressing her body against his naked torso. He sucked harder, hungrier, until the torment of his lips and fingers was all her brain could still contain – until she knew nothing but him and the desperate need for him burning between her legs. Again she couldn't suppress a moan. Against her thigh his arousal stirred.

'Runo...'

Without an answer he released her nipples, hands wandering down and yanking her skirts aside as he positioned himself between her legs. Before she knew what was happening, his warm breath stroked over the wetness between.

"*Runo*! You—'

Then his mouth found her smouldering flesh, and hungry, incoherent ecstasy washed over her – a sensation of weightlessness, of infinite freedom. Oh, gods. She had to be dreaming after all – could anything real ever feel so deliriously good? His lips worked her with charged, focussed purpose, exploring her body gently at first, then devouring with untamed, unrelenting greed. He drank deep from her, drowned her in his fervour until every inch of her was burning, aching for release. Tamar wrapped her legs around his shoulders and tangled her fingers into his curls, guiding him to the most sensitive spot – so close – so, so close...

His tongue twisted over her swollen flesh one more time, and she surrendered. Waves of relief pulsed through her, tearing her apart in the most pleasurable of ways; even her voice lost control of itself now, moaning his name in dazed, unfocussed gasps. Still he didn't pull back, didn't even buckle as she clenched her thighs around his body in mindless ecstasy. His lips continued nuzzling her, featherlight kisses that made her throbbing body clench up again and again until the high of the climax finally ebbed away, leaving nothing but an aching need for more of him, all of him. With every throb, every shiver, she only felt the emptiness, the absence of him inside her.

'Runo.' A hoarse whisper. 'I want you – so badly.'

'Oh, I know,' he said, looking up to smile at her – pure torture in a single expression. 'Don't worry, you'll get me. When I think you're ready for it.'

'When you...' She uttered a breathless laugh, then gasped as he lowered his face between her legs again and once more found that painfully pleasurable spot between her lips. 'You *bastard*!'

'Be careful,' he muttered, kissing her slit with quick, clever lips. 'I may just make you wait a little longer. Spent enough time looking forward to tasting—'

She swatted a hand at him, out of principle rather than honest conviction, then fell back into her blankets and clenched her fist into his curls when his tongue trailed along her aching wetness again. It didn't matter how hard she pushed or pulled, how tightly she clenched her thighs around his shoulders. He never even flinched. His tongue and lips persisted without mercy, kissing and licking and nuzzling until that unrelenting tension built in her once more, flowed into every tip of her toes and fingers and broke again in ripples of tingling light. She was laughing when she came to her senses, laughing and moaning, feeling like the least queenlike creature in the world, and delighting in the liberty of it.

'And believe me,' he whispered, coming up to kiss her, 'you were worth the wait.'

She wrapped her shaking hands around the back of his neck and pulled him closer until his muscular body lay pressed against hers. Through the rumpled mess of her skirt his erection was a beam of steel. His kiss tasted salty and sweet at once, lustful and reassuring, forbidden and inescapable – a promise, and one she could no longer deny. She let go of his neck to reach for his trousers, the linen still damp from the rain outside, and quickly undid his buttons. Only when she tried to pull his clothes off him did he stop her with a swift, unyielding hand around the wrist.

'Get out of that dress first, Your Majesty.'

Never had she freed herself from any dress so quickly. He pulled her closer as soon as the black silk slithered onto the floor, pinning her against his firm chest while his fingers stroked down to the wetness between her legs again. She wrestled to move but didn't win an inch on the iron hold of his arms around her waist – if anything, he held her tighter the harder she tried to free herself.

'Say it, Tamar.' She wasn't sure which of them enjoyed the struggle more; the grin on his face mirrored her own hunger, her own frenzy. 'Say please. See if you can convince me you really need me.'

'Go to hell,' she managed, wrestling down her laughter as much as her frustration. 'You've made me wait six weeks, you wretch – how dare you...'

'You should know by now I dare much more than is healthy for me,' he muttered, slipping a fingertip into her. Her entire body screamed for more at the touch, but he pulled back before she could arch closer. 'Be a little nicer, or I'll have to make another effort to persuade you...'

'You'll be the death of me after all – *oh*.' She gasped for breath as he sank the first inch of a finger into her again. 'Oh, gods – admit it, assassin. You're still trying to murder me, aren't you?'

'And enjoying it thoroughly.' He sniggered. 'But if you want something else from me, you only need to ask.'

'You *know* I want you,' she groaned, giving up her struggle at last. Red strands of hair hung before her eyes, and yet his handsome face, mere inches away, was still the clearest thing in the world. The bulge of his erection prodded her thigh, taunting her with its hardness. 'I'd have poisoned seven more husbands to get you back alive – is that what you want me to say? How much more do you want me to feed that arrogance of yours?'

He turned her on her back in the blankets, one hand still against her waist, the other yanking down his trousers. 'Only seven?'

'Perhaps an eighth if you'd stop being so damned insufferable,' she managed through her laughter. His hard length stroked along her inner thigh. 'Also, I promise you I'll drop dead if I don't get your cock inside me *now*. Is that what you want?'

He sniggered. 'One more word?'

'Oh, hell's sake – *please*.'

Then finally she felt his straining tip against her entrance, and the acute surge of sensations blotted the last of her coherent thoughts. Far, far away she still heard his golden voice, soft and teasing – 'That's all I needed to hear, Your Majesty...' But all of her senses focussed on his girth as he finally entered her, stretching her open, filling her deep. A satisfaction washed over her that seemed too large for her body to contain, a fullness, a *rightness*. Her body moulded to his as he sank into her, delighted in the newfound familiarity of him. Then he was in her, all of him, and only a single word found its way to her lips.

'Please...'

He slid half out of her, then thrust deep again, slamming the breath from her lungs. Claiming her. Controlling her. She could no longer tell if she felt pleasure or pain, hunger or helplessness; all sensations blurred into one nameless, faceless flood of passion as he fucked her, rough strokes rocking her body, filling her to the hilt again and again and again. Far too soon the tension rose in her anew, a pressure building higher and higher until she heard herself moan his name with every thrust, every breath falling over her lips...

She came in a blistering frenzy, legs tightening around his hips and fingers clenching to fists in his hair. Perhaps she moaned. Perhaps she screamed. For one soul-shattering heartbeat she existed only in a void, no longer aware of her own voice and mind and body – then she found herself back in her blankets, spent and shivering, Runo's arms tight around her, his seed sticking to her thigh. Her body sizzled. Her heart pounded against her ribs. But her mind was a cloudless summer sky, a blissful dream of nothingness, and she hadn't felt so little like iron in a decade.

'Pretty sure I'm dead,' she managed, snuggling up against his chest and pressing a kiss to the sweaty skin just under his collarbone. Under her lips his heart was racing too, but his quiet chuckle still came out calm and unfathomably reassuring.

'Look what it can do for you,' he whispered, 'saying please every now and then.'

She couldn't help but laugh – rosy giggles against his chest, like some silly little girl, some naive damsel unable to rein in a childish infatuation. And what did it matter if she was? Those tender, concentrated fingers combing through her hair didn't give the impression he'd think any less of her for it.

And only then did the full realisation hit her – that he wasn't running off again. That he'd stay with her. That she no longer had to be unyielding and unbreakable, not every moment of the day at least. That he'd keep her secrets. A Taavi assassin, of all people in the world, but how could she care about his past if this was the future he promised her?

She closed her eyes. Drank in the sensation of his presence, his safe, strong arms around her, and tried to believe it.

They lay in dark, lightheaded silence until the last flames in her hearth had flickered out and only the glow of the coals remained, just enough to distinguish the lines of his chest, the muscular ridges of his abdomen. Slowly the sensible thoughts seeped back into her mind. Tomorrow morning she'd have to smuggle him out of her room without the court noticing. Explain his sudden reappearance to Amiran and Terenti. Prepare for all the Empress might do if she found out her assassin had emerged as a guest at the Red Castle...

But she laid her hand on his warm chest and felt the slow beat of his heart below, felt his arms around her, keeping her safer than any iron mask had ever done. Tomorrow morning was ages away. Right now there was just him. All his utter madness. All his intoxicating freedom. The two of them against the rest of the world, after all.

Slowly her thoughts wandered off into the territory of dreams. She still noticed him tugging a blanket over her, still noticed his lips on the crown of her head. His voice drifted into her mind last, quiet and fragile – 'Sleep well, Your Majesty...'

She breathed a drowsy laugh. 'Sleep well, assassin.'

Then she slept, deep and dreamless, as if she'd never know a dangerous day in her life again.

Tamar and Runo's story continues in book 2 of the trilogy, *Silver*. With a vengeful Empress after them, will the queen and the assassin be able to save their lives ... and their love?

OTHER BOOKS BY LISETTE MARSHALL

Are you looking for even more Five Kingdoms content? The **free** novella *The Spinster & The Thief* takes place a few years before *Iron* and tells the story of Zovinar of Tanglewood. You can find it via www.lisettemarshall.com/five-kingdoms (scroll all the way down).

The Princess & The Spy

She despises his coldness. He loathes her nosy questions. But to avoid a war, they have no choice but to work together...

When a rebellious princess joins forces with her father's cold, bitter spymaster to keep her kingdom safe, there is no denying the forbidden fire flaring up between them.

Court of Blood and Bindings

"They call him the Silent Death, because he kills without a sound and leaves none capable of speaking in his wake..."

When the empire's deadliest fae murderer catches her wielding forbidden magic, twenty-year-old Emelin believes her hour has come. Instead, he offers her a dangerous bargain.

Court of Blood and Bindings is the first book in the Fae Isles series, an epic fantasy romance featuring winged fae, powerful colour magic and passionate enemies to lovers romance.

About the Author

Lisette Marshall is a fantasy romance author, language nerd and cartography enthusiast. Having grown up on a steady diet of epic fantasy, regency romance and cosy mysteries, she now writes steamy, swoony stories with a generous sprinkle of murder.

Lisette lives in the Netherlands (yes, below sea level) with her boyfriend and the few house plants that miraculously survive her highly irregular watering regime. When she's not reading or writing, she can usually be found drawing fantasy maps, baking and eating too many chocolate cookies, or geeking out over Ancient Greek.

To get in touch, visit www.lisettemarshall.com, or follow @authorlisettemarshall on Instagram, where she spends way too much time looking at pretty book pictures.

9 789083 256832